P.R.

Praise for Maureen Lee

'You'll be totally gripped by this wonderful tale' *Woman's Own*

'Maureen Lee is one of those hugely talented authors who writes great women for women readers. Her books don't just have one heroine, they have several' *Daily Record*

'With her talent for storytelling, queen of saga-writing Maureen Lee weaves intrigue, love and warmth into every page' *My Weekly*

'Big on drama and there's enough excitement packed into these pages to last a lifetime' *Now Magazine*

'Should keep you reading till the sun goes down. Packed with all the right ingredients – love, tragedy and the heroine's indomitable will to survive' *Woman's Realm*

Maureen Lee was born in Bootle and now lives in Colchester, Essex. She is the author of several bestselling novels, and has also had numerous short stories published and a play staged. Her novel *Dancing in the Dark* won the 2000 Parker Romantic Novel of the Year Award. Visit her website at www.maureenlee.co.uk.

By Maureen Lee

Lights Out Liverpool
Put Out the Fires
Through the Storm
Stepping Stones
Liverpool Annie
Dancing in the Dark
The Girl from Barefoot House
Laceys of Liverpool
The House by Princes Park
Lime Street Blues
Queen of the Mersey
The Old House on the Corner
The September Girls
Kitty and Her Sisters
The Leaving of Liverpool

A Dream
Come True

Maureen Lee

An Orion paperback
First published in Great Britain in 2007
by Orion Books Ltd
Orion House, 5 Upper St Martin's Lane,
London WC2H 9EA

3 5 7 9 10 8 6 4 2

Quick Reads™ used under licence

A CIP catalogue record for this book
is available from the British Library.

ISBN 978 0 7528 8239 0

Typeset by Deltatype Ltd, Birkenhead, Merseyside
Printed and bound in Great Britain by
Mackays of Chatham plc, Chatham, Kent

The Orion Publishing Group's policy is to use papers that
are natural, renewable and recyclable products and
made from wood grown in sustainable forests. The logging
and manufacturing processes are expected to conform to
the environmental regulations of the country of origin.

www.orionbooks.co.uk

For my agent, Juliet Burton

A Dream Come True

CHAPTER 1

It was Friday evening when Maggie phoned her husband from the conference hotel in Brighton.

'Hello, John, I've arrived safely,' she said in her quiet, gentle voice.

'Did you have a pleasant journey, dear?' he asked politely.

You'd never think they'd been married for over twenty years. 'Fine, thank you,' she replied, just as politely. 'I got here just in time for dinner.'

'I hope you enjoy the weekend, Margaret.' He was the only person who called her by her full name. 'Sleep well tonight.'

They said goodbye and rang off. Maggie put on more lipstick and combed her thick brown hair, looking critically at herself in the mirror. Her eyes were grey with flecks of silver and her skin was flawless, if a bit pale. She was quite attractive, despite her ordinary white blouse, black skirt and sensible low-heeled shoes. Neither tall nor short, Maggie looked older than forty-three – or at least she thought so. It was a

long time since anyone had paid her a compli-
ment. There'd been a time when people had
told her she was pretty – John used to tell her
all the time – and in those days she'd *felt* pretty,
too, but she didn't feel it now.

She went along the corridors and down the
stairs to the dining room, her feet sinking into
the thick carpets. Maggie hadn't stayed in
many four-star hotels.

'Are you dining alone, madam?' a waiter
asked when she entered the dining room.

'Yes.'

Her boss, Hugh Miller, wasn't expected until
later that night. Maggie worked in Liverpool for
Astral Travel Agency, which had recently been
taken over by a big London company. Buzz, as
it was called, had been buying agencies all over
the country and now owned one in every big
town and city. Felix Anderson, the founder,
was quite famous – Maggie had often seen him
on television. Now that they were all one
company he had made arrangements for this
weekend conference, to which staff from all the
agencies had been invited, so that he could talk
about the future, and tell them how he wanted
the business to be run.

'I suppose we'll all learn our fate tomorrow,'
Hugh had said gloomily the previous day. He
was worried that Felix Anderson would employ

his own staff at the agency and he would lose his job.

After she'd eaten, Maggie went for a walk along the brightly lit Brighton seafront. By now, it was dark, but warm for October. She was aware that she was one of the few people who were there on their own and for some reason she felt tears prick her eyes. If only things were different between her and John! If only she could telephone and tell him how lonely she was – not just tonight, but most nights. She felt lonely even when they were in the same room. Over the last few years, they'd grown further and further apart.

She was leaning against the railing, listening to the sound of the sea, when a voice said, 'Excuse me.'

Maggie turned to see a young man with fair hair and deep blue eyes, who was smiling broadly at her. 'Yes?' she replied.

'You're staying at the Brighton Towers, aren't you? I sat near you in the dining room. Are you here for the Buzz meeting too?' Maggie nodded and he went on, 'I wondered whether I could invite you to have a drink with me?' His smile became even broader. 'I'd rather not be on my own. If I go into pubs by myself, I only get hassled by people who think I must be in need of company. It must be my fatal attraction!'

Maggie felt her lips curl into a smile. He was charming and handsome. About six feet tall, he wore jeans and a leather jacket.

'All right,' she agreed, 'though I don't normally go into pubs with strange men.'

He thrust out his hand. 'I'm Connor O'Reilly from Manchester, married with three children. There now, you know my name so I'm no longer a stranger.'

'Maggie Holt from Liverpool. I'm married, but have no children.' They shook hands. No one, not even John, knew how much it hurt her to say that she had no children. 'You hardly look old enough to be married with a family,' she remarked.

'I'm thirty-five.'

'You don't look it.' He was only eight years younger than she was.

'I don't know what age you are, but you don't look it either.'

They grinned at each other. Maggie thought it was a miracle that he'd come along when he had, just when she really needed company.

They entered the first pub they came to and, although it was full of customers, they managed to squeeze themselves on to the end of a bench. Maggie felt very daring and couldn't recall when she'd last been out with a man who wasn't her husband. She told herself that she wasn't exactly going out with Connor.

He went to the bar and brought back a glass of white wine for her and half a pint of lager for himself.

'What does your husband do?' he asked as he sat down again.

'He's a teacher, a headmaster. Does your wife work?' That seemed a silly question to ask when he'd told her that she had three children, which must mean she had lots of work to do at home, but Connor nodded.

'Emma's a secretary.' A shadow fell over his boyish face. 'Her mother looks after the children during the day, but I worry about our son, Harry. He's three and a real handful, always on the go. Emma's mother doesn't have much patience with him.' He shrugged. 'Mind you, neither does Emma, so what difference does it make?'

If Maggie had three children, she'd want to be with them every minute of every day, no matter what they were like. John, a very religious man, had refused to be tested to see whether it was he who could not have children. The doctor had found nothing wrong with Maggie that would explain why she had not become pregnant.

5

'If it's what God wants, then who am I to argue with Him?' John had said.

'But why on earth would God not want us to have children?' Maggie had cried.

John didn't answer, and she wondered if that was because he didn't want people to know the fault was his.

Connor asked whether she was worried that Felix Anderson might tell them that some people would lose their jobs when he spoke to them the following day.

Maggie said, 'It wouldn't bother me if I did. I only work part-time. If I lose this job, I can easily get something else. It's a different matter for my boss though, so I am worried about him.' She'd worked with Hugh now for ten years. As he was in his late fifties, it would be much harder for him if he found himself out of work. 'What about you?' she asked Connor.

'My agency, Centurion, was started by my great-grandfather almost a hundred years ago,' he explained. 'When Buzz offered to buy the business, I wanted to keep it but Emma insisted I sell. She was dazzled by the amount of money Buzz offered.' He frowned. 'Now my job's at risk and she's concerned because she knows the money that we got from the sale won't last for ever.'

Maggie got the distinct impression that his

marriage was an unhappy one. Whenever he spoke about Emma his smile disappeared. She vowed not to mention his family again and changed the subject. 'What do you think of Brighton?'

'It's a great place, full of life. Not that Manchester's exactly dull.'

'Neither is Liverpool, although my favourite place in the world is Paris.' She and John had gone to Paris on their honeymoon. 'Have you ever been?'

'Many times, but *my* favourite place is New York.' His blue eyes danced. 'Have *you* ever been?'

Maggie giggled. 'No. What's your favourite film? Mine's *Scent of a Woman* with Al Pacino.'

'Mine's *The Shawshank Redemption*. Which television soap do you like best? I never miss *EastEnders*.'

Maggie had to confess that she never watched the soaps. 'John can't stand them. He keeps the remote control on the arm of his chair, so they're off limits.'

They compared likes and dislikes and, after about ten minutes, they found that they had nothing at all in common. 'Ah, never mind, Maggie,' Connor said with his lovely grin. 'We like each other. At least, I like you.'

'And I like you,' Maggie said warmly – more warmly than she'd intended. She blushed.

'Would you like to see the pier?'

She clapped her hands like a child. 'Yes, *please*.'

'Come on then.'

When he took her hand, she didn't pull away, but let him lead her outside and back to the seafront. By now, it was even darker, and the pier, shining brilliantly with lights of every colour, stretched away into the black water.

'It's beautiful,' Maggie gasped.

'Not bad, is it?' Connor was still holding her hand as they strolled along. Suddenly, he stopped dead and said quietly, 'I've only been with you for a few hours and yet I feel as if I have known you for years. As if I have always known you.'

'I know,' she murmured. 'I feel the same.'

Maggie thought it was like being in a dream, except she'd never dreamt that something like this would ever happen. She wasn't even sure what *was* happening – but for now, she knew she was happy.

They stood and watched the thin curve of new moon that had appeared from behind a cloud. 'Aren't you supposed to make a wish if you see a new moon?' Connor asked.

'I'm not sure,' Maggie admitted. 'It might

have to be a full moon, but shall we make a wish just in case?'

'I reckon we should.'

For a moment, they were silent as they stared at the moon, surrounded by a million tiny stars. She had no idea what Connor wished, but Maggie wished that the weekend in Brighton would be the best she had ever known.

CHAPTER 2

WHEN MAGGIE WOKE UP, there was a man in the bathroom singing at the top of his voice.

She took a moment to recognise who it was. Connor! She could hardly believe it. Last night everything had moved so quickly, but she'd been happy to forget about her worries and just enjoy being with Connor. When they got back to the hotel, it had seemed perfectly natural for him to come back to her room with her. There'd been no need for him to ask – and she and Connor had spent the night together. It wasn't like her at all but, for the first time in her life, she'd been unfaithful to her husband.

Maggie felt herself flush with embarrassment and guilt that she had betrayed John, yet her heart turned over at the memory of what it had been like making love with Connor. It had been truly fantastic, like nothing she'd experienced before.

He came out of the bathroom now, a towel wrapped around his narrow hips. 'Good morning,' he murmured when he saw that she was awake. He leant over the bed and kissed her, his hair wet, his skin smelling of soap.

10

'Good morning,' Maggie said in a whisper. Last night, they'd been as close to each other as a man and woman could be, but now she didn't know what to say to him or how to behave.

'Would you like tea or coffee? There's milk and stuff here, and I've boiled the kettle.' His smile lit up the room.

'Tea, please.' Maggie sat up and quickly tucked the bedding around her, feeling shy when she realised that she had nothing on. Looking for her clothes, she saw them thrown untidily over the back of a chair. That was unlike her, too.

Connor brought two mugs of tea and sat beside her on the bed.

'This seems so unreal,' Maggie said. 'I've never done this sort of thing before.'

'I didn't think you had,' Connor said softly. 'Neither have I. Since I met Emma, I haven't looked at another woman – until I saw you.'

Maggie didn't reply, yet she wanted to ask, What's so special about me? What do you see in me? It was a long time since a man had looked at her twice.

Connor seemed to sense her unease and gave her a gentle smile, before taking the mug of tea out of her hands and putting it on the bedside table. 'I'm starving,' he said.

11

'They'll be serving breakfast soon,' she reminded him, but Connor just grinned.

'Not all that soon.'

'What do you mean?'

'This!' He pulled the bedclothes away. Then he undid the towel around his waist and kissed her very, very slowly. Maggie's head began to whirl as his hands stroked her body and she was completely lost in the moment, unable to think about anything else . . .

The meeting was being held in the hotel ballroom. Maggie and Connor were the last to arrive and people looked up when they came through the door. Maggie hoped she wasn't blushing as Connor made for two empty seats and everyone had to stand up to let them through.

They'd hardly been seated a minute when a man came on the stage. It wasn't Felix Anderson – Maggie would have recognised him. This man was short and stout. He had very little hair and a shiny pink scalp. He explained why Felix Anderson had bought so many agencies. He said it was because one big company could offer holidays more cheaply than a group of little ones. Running costs would be lower if fewer staff were required. At this, some people groaned because if Buzz needed fewer staff it meant that some of them would lose their jobs.

As the talk didn't interest her, Maggie let her mind wander. She looked around for Hugh Miller, her boss, and spied him on the far side of the room. Hugh had once had ginger hair, but now it was silver grey. It was odd the way his eyebrows hadn't changed colour. She thought he looked a bit sick.

Maggie had worked at Astral longer than anyone but him and they were good friends, which was why he had chosen to invite her to the Brighton conference. 'I've been sent invitations for two,' he had explained. Men were expected to bring their wives, and wives their husbands, but Hugh and his wife had been divorced a long time ago and he had no one to bring. 'Why not enjoy a free weekend away in a posh hotel, Mags?' he'd suggested. 'If I ask one of the girls, the other three will tear her hair out.'

By 'the girls' he meant the booking clerks, who were all blonde and glamorous.

She could feel Connor O'Reilly's arm pressing against hers and sensed a warmth between them. She wondered whether he'd invited Emma to come with him and she'd refused.

People around her began to clap and Maggie realised with a start that the talk had finished.

13

Connor also seemed to have been lost in thought. They smiled at each other and began to clap too.

In the coffee interval Hugh came over to them. 'You look well, Mags. The Brighton air has already done you good.'

She introduced him to Connor. 'We met last night,' she said, as coolly as she could manage.

Felix Anderson spoke after coffee. He was slimmer and more handsome than he looked on television and his suntan was the deepest Maggie had ever seen on anyone. After welcoming everyone to Buzz, he promised that none of the managers would lose their jobs, adding, 'As long as they understand everything there is to understand about computers.'

Across the room, Maggie saw Hugh make a face. He was hopeless with computers and could barely type. As soon as they got back to Liverpool, she'd give him some lessons.

In the afternoon, they were shown a film all about Buzz. The company were buying chains of hotels all over the world. It owned hire-car firms, gambling casinos, restaurants and night-clubs. Felix, their new boss, appeared on the screen looking even more tanned than ever. He said that he was in the process of starting his own airline. In the not too distant future, people who booked a Buzz holiday would fly on a Buzz plane, hire a Buzz car, stay in a Buzz hotel and eat in a Buzz restaurant.

He then announced that, each month, the names of two Buzz employees would be chosen at random and they would win a weekend break anywhere in Europe. Maggie imagined going to Paris with Connor for a weekend, just the two of them. It would be sheer magic.

When the film was over, everyone went off to get ready for dinner.

Alone in her room, Maggie wished she had something nicer to wear. All she'd brought with her was another very ordinary blouse and skirt, similar to the ones she was wearing now. She looked at her watch. It was a quarter to five. As dinner wasn't until half past six, there would still be time enough to shop. She grabbed her coat and bag, and left the hotel.

Only a short walk away she found a main road full of shops and went into the first big store she came to. Following signs to the department she wanted, she was soon wandering through the rows of lovely dresses, skirts and blouses. She chewed her lip, knowing she didn't have much time to pick and choose. Should she buy the green frilly skirt or the brown silky one? She tried on both and decided that the brown suited her best as it showed off her slim figure. Now what she needed was a

15

pretty top to go with it. She grabbed a lacy cream blouse, paid for that and the skirt, then raced to the shoe department for a pair of sandals. Feeling reckless, she bought gold ones.

Connor's face was a picture when they met for dinner that night and Maggie could see the admiration in his eyes. She knew she looked her best in the new clothes. In fact, the woman who had stared back at her from the mirror in her bedroom had looked very different to the one the night before. This woman had rosy cheeks and bright eyes, and even her hair somehow looked shinier.

Connor said little because Hugh was at their table and he stayed with them when they went to the bar after dinner for a drink. Maggie didn't mind. After all, Hugh had asked her to Brighton and he was a friend. She wouldn't dream of trying to avoid him.

Hugh was the first to say he was going to bed so Maggie and Connor let a few minutes pass before they went upstairs themselves. Maggie's heart was beating like a drum. This was the moment she'd been waiting for all day. She handed Connor the key to her door. He opened it and stood aside to let her in.

This would be their last night with each other. The meeting would finish at noon

16

tomorrow, everyone would go home, and Maggie would be left with just the memory of Connor and the wonderful time they'd had together.

CHAPTER 3

MAGGIE DIDN'T LIKE DRIVING long distances. She'd come to Brighton on the train and was glad when Hugh offered to drive her back to Liverpool. It would be nice to have someone to talk to. Besides, if she went home by train, it would be useless trying to read the book she'd brought with her. She knew she wouldn't be able to stop thinking about Connor.

As far as Maggie was concerned, their relationship was over because it had no future. Meeting Connor had done her the world of good, making her feel young and pretty again, but she knew she couldn't be the sort of woman who had affairs behind her husband's back. But as Maggie watched the scenery flashing by and tried to concentrate on what Hugh was saying, she felt that she wasn't at all sure whether she wanted to return to her old, rather boring life.

Connor had said he'd telephone her at work.

'But what good will that do?' she had asked.

'If I telephone, it means I will hear your voice,' Connor had replied. 'One day we will meet again. We *have* to.'

There had been tears in his eyes as well as hers. Maggie's heart had felt as if it would break when they kissed for the final time. The affair had been amazing while it had lasted – she'd needed him at exactly the same time as he'd needed her – but it was definitely over, no matter what Connor might say.

Maggie suddenly realised that she hadn't heard a word Hugh had just said, so she tried hard to put Connor out of her mind and pay attention to her boss. Hugh seemed very fed up, convinced that he would lose his job. When Felix Anderson had spoken to them both that morning, Hugh had the feeling that Felix hadn't liked him one bit. 'He thinks I'm a wimp. He wanted to know why Astral didn't open on Sundays and stay open till late some nights. What did he say to you?' he asked Maggie.

'Not much – once I'd told him I only worked part-time. We only had a brief chat, really.'

'He liked you. He told me that he liked you,' Hugh said sulkily.

He sulked for the rest of the way home and Maggie almost wished she'd gone by train after all. She was relieved when they reached Liverpool, by which time it was dark, and she was even more relieved when they stopped outside the detached house in Crosby where she and John had lived for the past twelve years.

'Thank you for the lift home.' She squeezed Hugh's hand. 'Try not to worry. I'm sure everything's going to be all right.'

'It's easy for you to talk. Felix Anderson liked you.'

Maggie didn't give a damn whether Felix Anderson liked her or not. She tried to console him. 'I'm sure he liked you too.' She felt sorry for Hugh. Being divorced and with his only relative living in Canada, he had to go home to an empty house. He was probably even lonelier than she was.

John, who must have heard the car stop, had opened the front door, and their dog, Amber, a golden Labrador, came galloping out to meet her.

'Are those clothes new?' John asked when she went indoors and took off her coat. Amber danced around her, delighted to have her back.

'I didn't think you'd notice,' she said. 'I bought them in Brighton. The other women were much better dressed than I was. Hello, pest.' She patted Amber's head fondly. 'Have you missed me?' The dog licked her new sandals.

'I only noticed because you don't usually dress like that,' John said. 'Your clothes are always very practical.' He took her suitcase and kissed her briefly on the cheek. He was a tall man, not quite fifty, with stooped shoulders and thinning hair. Recently, he'd started to wear glasses all the time.

'Oh, John!' Maggie buried her head in his shoulder. She felt so guilty. He was a kind man, very gentle, who wouldn't have hurt a fly, yet she hadn't given him a thought when she'd made love with Connor.

'There, dear.' He clumsily patted her back and Maggie could tell she was making him feel ill at ease. She moved away and saw relief on his face. 'The estate agent looking after your mother's flat called,' he told her. 'They said that the new tenants who were going to take it have now withdrawn. It seems they want something larger. The agents are trying to let the flat again.'

'That's a pity.'

Eleven years ago, Maggie's beloved mother had died after a long illness. She'd lived in a flat on the seafront less than a mile away with stunning views over the River Mersey. After her mother's death, Maggie couldn't bring herself to sell the place. It was so much nicer than their modern house and she'd always secretly hoped that one day she and John would live there.

21

She'd never said anything to him about it – he would probably think it was a crazy idea.

'Would you like some supper?' she asked.

'No, thank you, dear. I think I'll go to bed. I have a busy day tomorrow.' As he was the headmaster of a state school, all his days were busy, but Mondays were the busiest of all.

Maggie glanced at the clock. It was only half past nine and she hated going to bed early. There had been a time when she and John had never gone to bed before midnight. In those days, they used to run upstairs and make love, but now they didn't even sleep in the same room, let alone the same bed. For the hundredth time she wondered what had happened to them?

John headed upstairs to bed and Maggie went into the kitchen where she made a sandwich. Amber begged for a slice of ham, which Maggie gave her. Now that John had gone, all she could think about was Connor. What was he doing right now? she wondered. He'd been worried about Harry, his youngest son. Over the weekend, he'd telephoned home quite a few times, wanting to make sure that Harry wasn't getting on Emma's nerves.

'He'd try the patience of a saint,' Connor admitted. 'He's got enough energy for half a dozen kids. Emma wants to calm him down with drugs but I think that's a terrible idea.'

'It's awful,' Maggie agreed. 'Harry sounds as if he's just full of beans. It would be a shame to drug him.'

She took the sandwich and a cup of tea into the living room, Amber following at her heels. It felt chilly so she switched on the electric fire. The dog collapsed on the rug, hogging the warmth of the fire, and immediately fell asleep. The room was as clean as a room could be. She'd dusted and polished everywhere before she went to Brighton and now it struck her that the house didn't look lived in at all. All the furniture matched, and the cream curtains matched the cream cushion covers. It was cold and colourless. Maggie wished that a little boy like Harry would come and make the room a mess.

Her mother's flat was very different. Mum had bought things because she liked them, not because they matched other things. In the big room, the curtains were red, the carpet green, and the walls were covered with brightly col-oured paintings. Maggie decided there and then to bring some of the paintings home and hang them in this room. John wouldn't like them, but she didn't like empty walls and it was *her* house too. She gave in too easily.

23

Not only would she bring home the paintings, but she'd start watching *EastEnders*. It would be easy to imagine Connor listening to the same words at exactly the same time.

The phone rang and her heart leapt to her throat. Connor! She picked up the receiver and gave her number.

'Hi, Mags.' It was her friend, Tess. How stupid to think Connor would ring her at home when he didn't even know the number. 'How did things go in Brighton?'

'Very well, thank you.'

'Did you meet the famous Felix Anderson?'

'Yes, he was quite nice, actually.'

'He was on the telly this morning.' Tess chuckled. 'It seems he plans to have the biggest chain of travel agencies in the world. Good luck to him, I say.'

'How are the children?' Maggie asked.

Tess had two sons and two daughters in their late teens and early twenties. Not long after their fifteenth wedding anniversary, her husband, Bill, had been killed when his car had crashed into a tree. No one else was involved, but Bill had been drinking and Tess and the children had completely gone to pieces. Maggie had taken over, sorting out the funeral, making sure the children ate and went to school, and drying Tess's tears when it seemed as if they would never stop. Those tears could still fall when things were going badly in her life.

'The children are driving me mad.' Maggie imagined her friend grimacing at the other end of the line. She didn't mean what she said about the children – she adored them. 'Mark's decided to hitch-hike around the world,' she complained. 'I'm being serious, Mags, that's what he wants to do. And Olivia cried all weekend because that creep of a boyfriend dumped her. Ewan got engaged for the third time. I don't know what the situation is with Clare. I haven't seen her since Thursday and I keep getting messages to say she'll be home soon, but she doesn't come.'

Beneath Tess's complaining tone, Maggie could tell she was worried about her eldest daughter, who was expecting a child of her own in about six weeks' time. Much to her mother's annoyance, Clare flatly refused to reveal who the father was. Clare had always been a very self-possessed, confident young woman, but since her father's death she had become more and more secretive. Trying to get quite unimportant information out of Clare, let alone the identity of the father of her baby, was like getting blood out of a stone.

Maggie and Tess arranged to meet the next

day after work. 'So you can tell me about Brighton,' Tess said.

'There's nothing to tell.'

'Oh, I'm sure you'll have thought of something by then,' Tess said cheerily.

CHAPTER 4

HUGH WAS STILL SULKING when Maggie arrived at Astral on Monday. He was a moody man, inclined to take his feelings out on his staff, and Maggie found two of the booking clerks, Julie Parsons and Kirsty Doyle, in a state. Both girls were only in their teens and were good, steady workers, but now Julie was in tears and Kirsty was in a flaming temper.

'What's the matter?' Maggie asked.

'Mr Miller said that if we didn't pull our socks up he'd give us the sack,' Julie sobbed.

'Yet we haven't done anything wrong,' Kirsty said angrily. 'I was about to tell him what to do with his stupid job, but he went into his office before I could.'

'It's just Mr Miller in one of his moods,' she told them.

'It hardly seems fair to take it out on us,' Julie sniffed.

'You're right, it doesn't.'

Maggie went into Hugh's office. 'What's got into you?' she asked. She had known him long enough to be able to speak her mind. 'Julie and

Kirsty are very good workers. I can't think of a single reason for you to be so horrible to them.'

'When I came in, the pair of them were laughing like idiots over something,' he said curtly. 'I told them to calm down, and said that if they did it again, they'd be out of a job.'

'Were any customers present at the time?' Maggie enquired.

'No,' Hugh growled.

'So, we can't laugh at work any more?'

'Don't be silly, Mags.'

'I'm not being silly, Hugh.' She felt angry. There were times when Hugh could be really unpleasant. 'You're in a mood because you're worried you'll lose your job, so you threaten two young girls with losing theirs.' She didn't care how much she upset him.

He jumped to his feet. She had upset him. 'Now, look here, Maggie—' he began.

'Don't get on your high horse with me, Hugh Miller. I suggest you tell Kirsty and Julie that you're sorry for being so nasty. A box of chocolates each wouldn't hurt either. Just imagine what would happen if they decided to leave! We'd be really short of staff, and if customers came in and saw a queue, they'd just go to another agency. Word might get back to Felix Anderson that we can't cope, and he'd want to know why two staff left so suddenly.

28

You wouldn't want him to know why, would you, Hugh?'

'No, of course not.' He frowned and his ginger eyebrows met over his nose. Sighing heavily, he said, 'Okay, I'll go and buy those chocolates. I won't be long.'

Maggie breathed a sigh of relief and went into her office. It wasn't much bigger than a cupboard, with only just enough room for a computer desk and a chair. Unlike the other women, Maggie had no contact with the public. She worked from ten until three typing letters concerned with complaints and queries that couldn't be dealt with over the telephone. She preferred to work part-time rather than have a nine-to-five job. It meant she had the weekend to herself, instead of spending it trying to catch up on the housework.

Turning on her computer, she made a note to herself to give Hugh a typing lesson when he came back. Then she rested her chin in her hands and thought about Connor. Now that the weekend was over, it was hard to believe that it had been real. It felt more like a dream than ever. She put her fingers to the lips that Connor had kissed. She closed her eyes and could feel his mouth on hers.

'Hi, Maggie.' Carol Copley poked her head around the door. She was in her early thirties, with perfect make-up and blonde hair that shone like silk. Hugh always left her in charge when he was away. 'I heard you give our dear boss a good talking to. He deserved it.' Her tone changed. 'How did the weekend go? Did you meet Felix Anderson?'

Maggie described what Felix had said at the conference as best she could. 'I don't think things here will alter much. Oh, the front desk staff will be getting new uniforms. They're smart pale grey suits with red piping and a red blouse. You can choose trousers or a skirt.'

'That sounds great. Talking of clothes, Maggie, you look really nice in that outfit. My sister's got a skirt just the same.'

'Thank you.'

Maggie decided that, when she finished work that afternoon, she would go out and buy some more clothes. All she did with her wages was put them in the bank. From now on, she'd start spending them for a change.

When Maggie got home that evening after doing her shopping, the house was empty. She guessed that John was still at school. She changed into her new clothes and went out again to meet Tess at a café they both liked.

Tess, who was dark-haired, wore bright scarlet lipstick and her enormous dark eyes were outlined with black. Her dangling gold earrings danced about wildly when she moved her head, reminding Maggie of a gypsy. Tonight Maggie wore her new clothes – a vivid red skirt and a black top with red embroidery that made *her* look a bit like a gypsy. She'd bought another pair of shoes too – black suede with wedge heels – and a red bead necklace glittered around her neck. When she arrived, Tess was puffing away on a cigarette – she smoked like a chimney.

Tess gasped. 'You look fantastic! Is this really the same Maggie Holt I went to dinner with last week?'

'Don't be daft, Tess,' Maggie mumbled. She must have looked a terrible frump before.

'Something happened in Brighton, didn't it?' Tess's eyes narrowed. She blew out a cloud of smoke from her cigarette. 'You met a fellow, I can tell. Your cheeks are like roses and your eyes are sparkling. What was he like? Come on, Mags, describe him in detail.'

'Tess!' Maggie's face felt as if it was on fire. There was a long pause while Tess stared at her, waiting for an answer. 'Oh, all right, I did meet someone,' Maggie admitted after a while. 'I wasn't sure whether or not to tell you.'

'You didn't *need* to tell me, I could see straightaway from the way you look.'

'Does that mean John will guess?' Maggie felt

31

alarmed. John had already noticed her new clothes when she came back from Brighton.

'No, only me. We know each other too well!' They'd started school together at the age of five and had been friends ever since, helping each other through the good times and the bad in their lives. Maggie would have trusted Tess with her life. 'So, how old is he? What's his name?'

'His name's Connor and he's thirty-five. He's also married with a family. We're not seeing each other again, Tess. I'm not starting an affair or anything.'

Connor had said he would telephone, but that was all.

Maggie paused, stared keenly at her friend and said, 'I can tell things about you too, you know. You're worried about something.'

Tess's hands were knotted together so tightly that the knuckles were white. She shrugged. 'It's Clare. You know I told you I hadn't seen her since Thursday?' Maggie nodded. 'Well, she should have been back home today in time for work – she refuses to take her maternity leave, even though she's as big as a house with the baby. If I were in her position, I'd be ashamed to go out. Anyway, there's no sign of her and the other kids don't know where she is. She just took off without saying where she was going. I assumed she was going to one of her friends' houses. She keeps ringing and leaving messages to say she'll be home the next day, but she never comes.'

'Have you phoned the police?'

'Why? To tell them my heavily pregnant, twenty-three-year-old daughter has sort of disappeared, but she hasn't really because she telephones every day? No, Maggie, I haven't rung the police.' Tess looked on the verge of tears.

'I'm sure she'll come home any minute,' Maggie tried to reassure her.

'I suppose she will.' Tess sighed. 'It's at times like this that I realise just how much I miss Bill. He was always better with the girls than me. Clare might have confided in him.' She managed to raise a wan smile. 'Tell me more about Connor. That'll help take my mind off things for a while.'

So Maggie told her about Connor's little boy, Harry, and added that she didn't think that he and his wife were happily married. She also described how Hugh Miller had spent most of Saturday with them and half of Sunday. 'Yet he didn't guess that Connor and I were more than friends.'

When she arrived home, John had gone to bed. Amber was fast asleep in her basket in the kitchen and only woke up to lift her head, give Maggie a dozy look, then flop back to sleep.

Maggie had only seen John for a few minutes that morning. If things continued in this way, the time would surely come when they didn't see each other at all except at weekends.

CHAPTER 5

THAT NIGHT, MAGGIE DREAMT about Connor. They were in a little boat together, she was trailing her hand in the water and he was rowing. They were singing the song 'Somewhere Over the Rainbow'.

When she woke, she felt guilty again. It didn't seem right to dream about one man when you were married to another. She could hear John moving about downstairs, so she got out of bed and threw on her dressing gown.

She found John in the kitchen, freshly showered and shaved, and about to butter a slice of bread. Was it just her imagination that he didn't look particularly pleased to see her? 'Let me toast that,' she said.

'I haven't got the time,' he said curtly.

'Oh, John, sit down, it will only take a minute.' She picked up the bread and put it in the toaster. 'I wish you'd wake me when you get up. I'd make you a proper breakfast.'

'I couldn't eat a proper breakfast. A slice of bread is ample.' He sat down at the table and glanced at his watch. Amber sat underneath, hoping for a titbit.

'Remember when we were first married? We used to have massive breakfasts.' John had had to fry the eggs because she always broke the yolks.

'Time didn't matter so much in those days.' He rubbed his forehead tiredly. 'I was only an ordinary teacher. Now I'm the head and every minute counts.'

The toast popped up and Maggie buttered it. She remembered how much he liked strawberry jam. There was a jar in the fridge, so she took it out and quickly spread some on. 'Here you are.' The plate was placed in front of him. 'Would you like some tea?'

'Yes please. I've already made a pot.'

She poured them both tea and sat at the table with him. It was a long time since they'd breakfasted together. 'Shall we go somewhere on Saturday night?' she suggested. 'To the cinema or for a meal? Or even both? We could see the new Harry Potter film.'

He looked at her impatiently. 'I'd sooner not, Maggie. I'm really not in the mood. It'll be Christmas soon and I have so much to do at school. On Saturday afternoon we're starting rehearsals for the pantomime. This year it's *Jack and the Beanstalk* and we're so late starting that we're even having a rehearsal on Sunday too.'

Maggie felt hurt. 'Surely you won't be rehearsing all afternoon and evening as well?'

'Of course not,' he snapped. 'But you can't expect me to want to go out to see a film after such an exhausting day.'

'I've learnt to expect nothing at all from you these days, John,' she said miserably. 'You're more married to the school than you are to your wife.' She walked out of the room and was halfway up the stairs when he appeared in the hall.

'I'm sorry, Maggie,' he called, looking up at her. 'It's just that I'm so tired.'

'Perhaps you should get a tonic from the doctor.'

'You're right. I'll go and see him one of these days.' He struggled into his fawn anorak. 'Bye, dear. I shall probably be home late tonight.'

'Bye, John.'

Maggie sat on the stairs and watched him go. There'd been a time when she would have stood at the door with him, helped him with his coat, kissed him passionately. She rested her chin on her folded arms and told herself that she must stop thinking this way: once they would have done this, once they would have done that! As far as she and John were concerned, those lovely times were over and she'd just have to get used to the fact.

Amber sat at the bottom of the stairs and looked at her appealingly. Maggie raised her eyebrows. 'I suppose you want to go walkies?' At the word 'walkies', the dog excitedly ran to fetch her lead and Maggie went upstairs to shower and get dressed.

By the end of the week, Hugh was still in a mean mood. He snapped at everyone, including Maggie, which didn't bother her, but she was becoming annoyed by the unpleasant atmosphere all the time. Julie was always on the verge of tears and Kirsty said that if he spoke to her rudely again she'd leave on the spot.

'I don't have to put up with it. There are loads of other jobs available,' she said.

'It's horrible at home and horrible at work,' Maggie said to Tess next time they spoke on the phone. Tess's daughter, Clare, still hadn't come home. Although she had telephoned to say she was all right, she still refused to say where she was.

'You poor thing,' Tess said kindly to Maggie. 'Once upon a time, I used to think you and John were the ideal couple. You never rowed, but Bill and I were for ever at each other's throats.'

'John and I don't see enough of each other to row much,' Maggie said dryly.

The next day, Friday, Connor telephoned. Although he'd said he would, Maggie hadn't really expected him to and, in a way, she had been glad that so far she hadn't heard from him. They had no future together and she would prefer him to remain a wonderful memory, even though she knew that it would get fainter and fainter as the years passed.

Despite her resolve, Maggie's heart turned over when Carol poked her head around the door and said, 'There's a call for you, Mags. It's some chap who says he's from Centurion in Manchester.'

'Thank you.' Maggie waited until Carol had gone before picking up the receiver. 'Hello,' she whispered.

'Maggie! How are you?'

'Fine, I'm fine, Connor. How are you?' Oh, it was lovely to hear his voice.

'I'm missing you. *Really* missing you, Maggie.' She imagined him sitting behind the desk in his office and wondered if the weather was as nice in Manchester as it was in Liverpool. Was the sun shining on him as it was on her?

'Is there somewhere we can meet?' Connor said.

39

'Oh, Connor, we can't.' She would have loved to meet him and stroll through the streets with him, her arm linked with his. Every now and then, she thought, he would lean down and kiss her. When night came, they would make love.

'Why can't we?' he asked.

'Because . . . because – oh, for all sorts of reasons. You're married. I'm married. You've got children. What point is there in us meeting, Connor?'

'Because I want to see you,' he said simply. 'And I thought you'd want to see me.'

'Oh, I would, I would,' she breathed.

'Then let's do it. Sunday, say?'

'Sunday?' It was so soon.

'Emma is taking the children to a party. They'll be out for most of the day. It will only take an hour for me to drive to Liverpool. What about you? Can you get away?'

'Yes.' She'd tell John she was going to see Tess. Her friend would be only too pleased to cover for her. 'How well do you know Liver-pool?'

'Reasonably well.'

'There's a restaurant at the bottom of Bold Street. It's called the Life Café. I'll see you upstairs.' The upstairs area was more private and it was unlikely that anyone she knew would be there. 'What time?' she asked.

'Three o'clock?'

'Three o'clock it is.' She put down the phone. When she looked up, Hugh Miller was watching from the doorway.

'Who was that?' he asked.

'A friend,' Maggie replied. 'Just a friend.'

She couldn't help but wonder how much he'd heard, but what did it matter if he'd heard the whole conversation? It was her business and hers alone.

CHAPTER 6

CONNOR WAS ALREADY AT the café when Maggie climbed the stairs. He wore jeans and the leather jacket he'd worn in Brighton. There were only two other couples there. His blue eyes lit up when she approached and she caught her breath – she had forgotten just how handsome he was.

'Maggie!' He stood up, took her in his arms and kissed her on the lips.

'Hello, Connor.'

It was so long since anyone had greeted her in that way that Maggie wanted to cry. When she sat down at the table, he took both her hands in his and kissed them, first the right and then the left.

'It's so good to see you again,' he murmured. 'I only wish there was somewhere even more private that we could go . . .'

Maggie knew what he meant and felt her insides shiver. Yet again she wondered what he saw in her. 'There isn't the time,' she said, reluctantly.

'I know.' He gave a little nod. 'I can't help but wonder if there ever will be.' He released her hands and began to caress her face, her neck, her hair. In his own way, he was making love to her in public. 'You have the gentlest eyes I've ever seen. That's what drew me to you in Brighton, your eyes. I could tell straightaway that you would never hurt me.'

'Why would anyone want to hurt you, Connor?'

'It's what a lot of people do to each other.' His mouth twisted bitterly.

'Does Emma hurt you?'

He shrugged. 'Sometimes.'

'Do you ever hurt her?'

He shrugged again. 'I don't know. These days, Emma and I are more like enemies than friends. We never seem to agree on anything that matters.'

The waitress came and they each ordered coffee and a sandwich.

'Is Harry the main thing that you disagree about?' Maggie asked when the waitress had gone.

His blue eyes darkened. 'Until Harry was born, Emma and I got along just fine. I get angry about the way she treats him – she's so impatient with him. Her mother is too.' His eyes filled with tears. 'Oh, Maggie, what am I going to do?'

'I don't know, Connor. I really don't know. What about your other children?'

He had a daughter and another son, both older than Harry, who were at school. He hardly ever spoke about them. Harry seemed to occupy his mind, which Maggie understood completely.

'Kate and Charlie are just two average kids. They're doing okay at school. Emma and I have no problem with them. It's just Harry . . .' He made a face. 'I'm sorry, Maggie. I didn't come all this way to complain. Let's talk about us, you and me – and Felix Anderson.' He grinned. 'Have you heard from him since Brighton?'

'No, not a word.'

'I got an e-mail confirming that I shall remain manager of what was my own agency! Didn't Hugh get one?'

'If he did, he hasn't mentioned it.'

She felt sure Hugh would have told her if he'd heard he was keeping his job. He was terribly worried about losing it. Unlike Connor, Hugh hadn't owned the agency before it was taken over by Buzz. It had belonged to an old Liverpool family and Hugh had merely been an employee.

The coffee and sandwiches arrived and they began to talk about more ordinary things. She told him she'd started to watch *EastEnders*.

They discussed the latest news. He said he was thinking of getting Emma a bigger car. 'The children are a bit squashed on the back seat of our present one.'

The time raced by. They ordered more coffee and, after they'd finished it, Connor said he must go. 'Emma will be back from the party soon. I hope Harry didn't do anything to annoy her,' he said, frowning. 'She keeps threatening to take him to the doctor. I think I told you she wants him to have tablets to quieten him down.'

'Yes, you did.'

She walked back to the car park with him. His car was in a dark corner of the garage and when they stopped next to it he kissed her long and hard. Then he got in the car and drove away.

Maggie felt terribly sad as she went to collect her own car. If Connor could get away, she had agreed to meet him at the same time and place the following Sunday. It would mean lying to John again, something she hated doing, but Connor needed her and Maggie was now determined to be there for him when she could.

Instead of driving straight home, she went to see Tess. It was where she had told John she would spend the afternoon. The house throbbed with noise and was so untidy that it looked as if a hurricane had swept through it. The children had invited their friends round. Two different sorts of music came from upstairs: James Blunt singing 'You're Beautiful' and something she didn't recognise, but which sounded like New Orleans jazz. In the lounge, some young people she'd never seen before were watching a scary video with the volume turned up high.

Tess was in the kitchen typing away on her laptop computer, going through the accounts work that she did from home for half a dozen different companies. A cigarette stuck out from the corner of her mouth.

'John called,' she informed Maggie. 'He said he'd rung your mobile, but found you'd left it upstairs. I told him you'd gone to Liverpool city centre to do some shopping.'

'Thanks, Tess.' Maggie had left her mobile at home on purpose. She hadn't wanted it to ring while she was with Connor. 'Did John say what he wanted?'

'No. Only that it wasn't important.'

'Have you heard any more from Clare?' Maggie asked.

'Yes.' Tess blew a perfect smoke ring. 'She's coming home tomorrow. I keep wondering whether she's married that Swedish chap that she's been seeing – Dirk something or other. I think he might be the father of her baby, but of course she won't tell me whether he is or not.' Tess stubbed out the cigarette and immediately lit another. 'Sometimes I think she doesn't even know herself who the father is – young people today are entirely lacking in morals.'

'But why would she leave home to get married?'

'I've no idea. Kids are mysterious beings, Mags. I'll never understand them.' She got up to put the kettle on. 'Now, tell me how you got on with Connor . . .'

When Maggie arrived home the place felt unnaturally quiet after the din in Tess's house. John was studying papers spread out on the dining-room table. Amber strolled across and stood waiting to be stroked.

'This is next term's timetable,' John explained. 'I've nearly finished. The table will be clear in a minute.'

'It doesn't matter,' Maggie said, 'we can have dinner in the kitchen. What time would you like to eat?'

'As soon as possible. I'm quite hungry.'

'I can have it ready straightaway.' She'd made a beef casserole before she went out and it was on a low heat in the oven.

'Did you buy anything in town?' he asked.

Maggie forgot for the moment that Tess had said she'd gone shopping, but she remembered just in time. 'I need a winter coat, but couldn't see anything I liked. I might go again next Sunday.' She really hated lying to him. He was a very honest person and she'd never known him to lie to her.

'I'm surprised that Tess didn't go with you.'

'She was waiting for a phone call from Clare. I told you she's been missing for over a week – anyway, she's coming home tomorrow.' Maggie took off her coat and hung it in the hall cupboard. 'Why did you telephone?' she asked when she returned to the room. 'I thought you were rehearsing the pantomime this afternoon?'

'It was a daft idea to do it on a Sunday,' he said, wrinkling his nose. 'Not enough kids turned up so it was called off. I thought we could have gone to see a film, but it's too late now.'

Maggie resented being fitted in because something more important had been cancelled, but she didn't say anything. Maybe John was trying to be nice. If so, it would be tactful for her to be nice back.

48

CHAPTER 7

As usual, John went to bed early and, feeling
restless, Maggie took Amber for a walk. Tonight
Amber decided to take charge, pulling Maggie
towards the river, and before long they were
passing her mother's flat. It was on the first
floor of a four-storey house with a long front
garden and its windows were the only ones in
darkness.

The keys for the flat were still on her keyring,
in her pocket. There had seemed no reason to
take them off. It meant that she was reminded
of her mother every time she let herself into her
own house or used the car. On a whim, she
went up the path and unlocked the front door.
Amber followed, sniffing noisily. She liked new
smells.

When she entered the hallway, Maggie realised that someone in the place was making a
curry, and Freddie Mercury was singing 'We are
the champions' behind the door of the ground-
floor flat. The building felt warm and lived in,
with flowers on the small table where the post
was left for people to collect.

Maggie climbed the carpeted stairs and

Amber galloped ahead. She had reached the second floor when Maggie had to call her back. 'We're going in here,' she said as she unlocked the door of her mother's flat.

She switched on the light. The room was like a colourful bazaar, with paintings that covered the walls and red silky curtains that shimmered. A silk tapestry decorated with sequins hung over the mantelpiece. As she looked around, Maggie realised she couldn't take anything there back to her own dreary house. It wouldn't be the right place for it. Mum's things belonged here, in her home.

Everything in the room brought back memories going as far back as her childhood. One of her favourite things was the glittering elephant with a bowl on its back. Her father, had been a merchant seaman and he had died when Maggie was five. He had brought the elephant home from India. Her mother used to keep fruit in the bowl but now it held dried leaves that had lost their scent. Another of Maggie's favourites was the ornate oval mirror, which had been given to her father as a wedding present and was now above the fireplace.

'Sometimes, I swear I can see your dad in it,' Mum used to say. Maggie, an only child, had looked and looked in the mirror, but had only ever seen herself.

One of her dearest memories of her father was of when he came home after a long absence. He would lift her high into the air so that she was looking down at him. She would squeal with delight and cry, 'What have you bought me this time, Daddy?'

'A present.' He'd put her back on the floor and tap the side of his nose. 'Would you like to see it?'

'Yes, *please*,' she would say.

Maggie remembered that in this way her father had given her a whole collection of china dolls from all over the world. 'I must look for them,' she murmured. 'I could put them on the dressing table in my bedroom.'

There was a box of her mother's smaller ornaments in the spare room back home. It held statues and vases, little fancy boxes and pretty bowls that she hadn't left in the flat in case the tenants broke them.

She picked up the phone and could hear that the line was still connected. She would have liked to call someone, but it was too late.

Amber had parked herself in front of the floor-length window. There was a balcony outside where her mother had sat in the summer. Maggie turned off the lights and sank into the comfortable chair in the window beside the dog. In the distance, the River Mersey glittered, the water reflecting the golden half-moon. A ship sailed by, brightly lit, on its way towards the Irish Sea and Maggie wondered what part of the world it was sailing to. The scene reminded her of strolling along Brighton seafront with Connor.

Maggie stretched out her legs and let her arms flop over the sides of the chair. It was peaceful here and the music from down below was just loud enough to hear. It was still Freddie Mercury, her favourite singer.

Tomorrow, she would get in touch with the estate agents and tell them she'd decided not to let the flat again. She really liked it here. 'We'll start coming here more often, shall we?' she said to Amber. The dog answered with a little bark.

'Did you have a good time yesterday?' Hugh asked when she arrived at work on Monday morning. He followed her into her office.

'Great,' Maggie replied vaguely. She was only half listening.

'What's that café like in Bold Street?'

'What café?'

'The one where you had a date. Three o'clock, I think you said it was.'

Maggie was listening now. She looked at him sharply. 'What are you talking about, Hugh?'

'On Saturday, I heard you make a date to meet someone. It was in a café in Bold Street. I just wondered what it was like. The café, that is, not the date.' His eyes were round and innocent, but she could tell that he was acting.

'I was meeting a friend, that's all. Do you make a habit of listening to other people's phone calls, Hugh?'

He laughed. It wasn't a very nice laugh, but Hugh hadn't been nice since they'd come back from Brighton. 'It was impossible *not* to listen, Mags. Your door was wide open.'

There was nothing Maggie could say to that. She sat behind her desk and hoped he would go away so that she could get on with some work. Instead, he closed her office door and sat down at the other side of the desk.

'I didn't know you and John were having problems,' he said.

Maggie gasped. 'How dare you say that? John and I are not having problems. I don't know what makes you think we are.'

'Perhaps it's the fact that you slept with Connor O'Reilly in Brighton.' His eyes gleamed nastily. 'Or perhaps I should say he slept with you. I saw him come out of your room on the Sunday morning. Then I saw you both in that café yesterday. That's not exactly the behaviour of a happily married woman, Maggie.'

She gasped again. 'You've been *spying* on me!'

He ignored that. 'Connor's too young for you – or you're too old for him, one or the other. What you need is a real man, Mags. How about me?'

Maggie half expected Hugh to beat his chest like Tarzan. She was too stunned to reply. All she wanted was for him to go away.

'I've always fancied you,' he continued in a low voice. The way he was looking at her made her feel sick. 'I've never done anything about it – I respect John too much for that – but if it's over between you and him, then I think you should give me a chance. After all, unlike Connor, I'm not married, and you and I could become permanent.'

'I don't think so, Hugh,' she said stiffly.

'Why not?' He was getting angry. 'What's wrong with me?' he demanded.

'Nothing. I'm sure loads of women would love to go out with you, but I'm afraid I'm not one of them.' She went over and opened the door. 'If you wouldn't mind, Hugh, I'd like to get on with some work.'

'I think you may have forgotten who's the boss here, Maggie.' Now he was really angry. 'No one orders *me* out of an office.'

'In that case, stay.' Maggie began to open the letters on her desk. She tried to appear calm on the outside, but her heart was beating wildly. In the ten years that she'd worked for Hugh, this was a side of him that she'd never seen.

She opened a big envelope and pulled out half a dozen glossy photos of stick-thin girls, clearly models, showing off the new grey uniform. There was also a letter asking for a list of the sizes required.

Maggie pushed past Hugh and took the photos into the outer office to show the girls. 'You'll be allowed two uniforms each,' she told them. 'They can be both the same, or you can have a trouser suit and a skirt suit. It's up to you.'

When she returned to her office, Hugh had gone.

'Thank goodness,' she breathed.

Tess phoned only a few minutes before Maggie was due to leave. 'Clare's home,' she announced.

'What has she been doing all this time?' Maggie asked.

'Come and see – call in on your way home.'

'Okay. I'll be with you in about half an hour.'

CHAPTER 8

EWAN, TESS'S YOUNGEST SON, opened the door to Maggie's knock. 'Hello,' he said grumpily. 'Mum's in the kitchen.'

'Congratulations.' Maggie patted him on the shoulder.

'What for?' He looked mystified.

'Your mum said you'd got engaged again.' She had the feeling that Tess had said that it was for the third time.

'Did she really?' Ewan said absent-mindedly without confirming whether it was true or not. He wandered upstairs while Maggie went into the kitchen to see her friend.

Tess was sitting by the table with a baby in her arms. She gave Maggie a dazzling smile. 'This is Susie,' she cried, 'my first grandchild.'

Maggie was so astonished that she sat down with a thump. 'I thought the baby wasn't due for another six weeks?'

'That's what Clare thought too, but she must have got her dates wrong. You know that she totally refused to see a doctor. She had labour pains the other day at her friend's house. The friend whisked her off to hospital and Susie was born. Clare was kept in there for a whole week because her blood pressure was too high.'

'But why didn't she let you know?'

'She said she wanted to surprise me.' Tess chuckled. 'But I reckon she didn't want me around, making a huge fuss and embarrassing her in front of the staff.' She looked fondly at her granddaughter. 'This little angel weighed seven and a half pounds. Don't you think she's gorgeous?'

Susie's blue eyes were wide open although she seemed to be staring at nothing. Her tiny hands opened and closed and her feet wriggled inside the white shawl that was wrapped around her tiny body. Her curly hair was the colour of butter.

'Really gorgeous,' Maggie agreed. She longed to hold the baby and held out her arms. 'Can I have her for a minute?'

'With pleasure.'

Tess put the baby in her arms. She felt as fragile as a bird. Her little feet continued to move and Maggie could feel her heels pressing against her left arm. Susie yawned, showing a mouth full of pink gum and, seconds later, she was asleep.

'I really wish John and I had had children,' she whispered, wishing she could have a little bundle of her own like this, or grown-up children like her friend's. She tried to imagine what it would feel like to become a grand-mother.

'Having children isn't all it's cracked up to be,' Tess said dryly. 'Clare's talking about going back to work in a few days' time and who do you think Susie will be left with? Her grandma, of course. The thing is, Mags, I'm forty-three years old, like you, and I've already raised four children. I reckon it's time I got some enjoy-ment out of life, rather than be stuck at home all day with a baby.'

'You could refuse to look after her,' Maggie suggested. 'Insist Clare does it herself.'

'All she'll do then is put Susie with a child-minder,' Tess said, looking angry. 'I'll feel torn between what to choose – my freedom or knowing my first grandchild is spending eight hours a day with a complete stranger. Child-minders probably have half a dozen other kids to look after at the same time.'

'You haven't really got a choice,' Maggie conceded.

'I know.'

'Imagine what our mothers would have said if one of us had turned up with a baby?'

'Mine would have skinned me alive.' Tess's parents lived across the water in Birkenhead. 'Even now, I'm quite likely to get a lecture from

Mum when she finds out about Susie. She'll accuse me of letting Clare have too much freedom.'

'My mum would have cried for a week, but she would have loved the baby.'

Tess laughed. 'Mine would have loved the baby too – *after* she'd skinned me alive.'

Maggie told John about Susie when he came home. 'She's such a dear little thing,' she said wistfully. 'I nursed her for ages. Clare let me give her a bottle.'

'There are two girls at school who are pregnant,' John told her. 'One's only fourteen. I'm not sure who I feel sorry for the most – the girls or their babies.'

Some people had babies so easily, it hardly seemed fair, Maggie thought. They had them, then gave them to other women to look after. She wondered whether her marriage to John would have been happier if they'd had children . . .

Maggie was busy typing letters when a round-eyed Carol came in to say that Felix Anderson was on the line. 'And he wants to speak to you, Maggie.'

Maggie picked up her phone. 'Good morning, Mr Anderson,' she said.

'Call me Felix. Didn't I tell everyone in
Brighton I want to be known by my first
name?'

'You did indeed – Felix.'

'That's better.' He sounded warm and
friendly. 'How are you today?'

'Very well, thank you. And how are you?'

'I'm full of the joys of spring.'

'It's October,' she reminded him. 'Almost
November.'

'In that case, I'm full of the joys of autumn.'
His voice changed, became harder. 'I'll come
straight to the point, Maggie. What do you say
to becoming manager of the Buzz Travel
Agency in Liverpool?'

'Do you mean *this* branch?'

'I do. Very soon, Astral Travel Agency will
become Buzz,' he said. Maggie was aware of the
excitement in his voice. 'Signwriters will come
and put the new name outside and the whole
place will be painted grey and red, both inside
and out. You'll have new furniture, new computers, new everything. And a new manager. I
don't expect you to make up your mind now,
Maggie, but I'd like to know by tomorrow.'

'What about Hugh Miller?' she asked.

'Hugh Miller isn't the sort of man that Buzz is
looking for. He has let things slide over the last
few years and Astral's profits have gone down

quite a lot. I know I shouldn't say this, but Hugh's a loser.'

When Felix Anderson rang off, Maggie wondered, does that mean I'm a winner?

Maggie was too busy to think about the job for the rest of the day. When she got home, she remembered that there was a Hallowe'en party at the school and John would be home even later than usual. Once upon a time, she'd attended all the school events. She'd gone to the concerts, the prize-givings and the sports days, but John hadn't invited her to anything at the school for ages.

She made herself a cup of tea and a sandwich and decided to take Amber for a walk. She'd visit her mother's flat. It would be easier to think there.

It was almost dark by the time she let herself into the house. Amber scrambled upstairs and remembered to stop outside the door on the first floor.

Maggie patted her head and told her she was a very clever dog. As soon as the door was opened, the dog made straight for the window and stood there, tail quivering. The road was busy, with cars sweeping past and children walking home from school.

A man of about forty walked up the path and

let himself in the front door. She heard him climb the stairs and enter the room on the top floor. Outside, a dog barked. Amber barked back and Maggie told her to shush.

She sat in the chair where she'd sat the other night. Straightaway, she began to relax and thought about Felix Anderson's offer. Did she really want to be the manager of a travel agency? When she was young, like most girls, she had wanted to do something exciting with her life. She'd imagined becoming an actress, a best-selling writer, reading the news on television.

She was eighteen when she had met John. He had been twenty, and they had fallen head over heels in love. He was grave and courteous with an old-fashioned charm and a lovely sense of humour, so different from the men she'd met before who seemed like silly boys in comparison. From then on, all she'd wanted was to marry him and start a family. She'd wanted four children, two boys and two girls, just like Tess. She'd already chosen their names – Daniel and Adam for the boys, Sophie and Ellen for the girls. She married John soon after meeting him and, while she waited for the children to arrive, she'd worked part-time in a bank as a typist.

But the children had never arrived. After

taking his degree, John put all his energies into his work and was promoted again and again until finally he was made a headmaster. As the years passed, he became so over-burdened with work that he lost all interest in everything outside the school, including her. Maggie had gone to work at Astral, a more interesting job than the bank. Now she was forty-three and had done nothing with her life.

She stared out of the window, watching the dusky sky darken. By now, there was even more traffic as people began to return from work. It came to her like a flash of light. She *didn't* want to manage a travel agency. She wanted to do something else, something really worthwhile – work with children, perhaps, or for a charity.

Tomorrow, she'd call Felix Anderson. She'd tell him she didn't want the job of manager. She'd say she was willing to stay with Astral until they found someone else to be manager, but that was all. It was a chance for a new beginning.

CHAPTER 9

THE FIRST THING THAT Maggie did when she got to work the following morning was to talk to Hugh. She hadn't spoken to him since yesterday when he'd been so horribly rude. Since then, he'd been shut in his office and Carol said he was there now. 'There hasn't been a peep out of him so far.'

Maggie knocked on the door and went inside. Hugh was staring at his computer screen, looking very pale.

'Is something wrong?' she asked.

'I found this when I turned on the machine this morning,' he said dully.

'What is it?'

'It's an e-mail from Felix Anderson saying that my services are no longer required. In other words, I've been given the sack.'

'Oh, Hugh! I'm so sorry.' She really was. They'd been good friends for a long time.

'What am I going to do, Maggie?' He sounded scared. There weren't many jobs around for a man of his age.

'I don't know.' She went over and squeezed

his shoulder. To her surprise, he reached up and caught her hand.

'I really do care for you, Maggie,' he said in a voice that trembled slightly. 'I'm sorry I was such a beast yesterday. If you ever decide to leave John, I hope you'll give me a chance.'

'I don't think so, Hugh.'

'What's wrong with me?'

He'd asked the same thing yesterday. 'Nothing,' she said patiently.

Carol came in. 'Felix Anderson is on the line for you, Maggie. Shall I transfer it to your office?'

'Please.'

'No,' Hugh barked. 'Transfer it here. Let's hear what he has to say.'

Carol looked at Maggie who gave a little nod. This wasn't the time to remind Hugh he'd just had an e-mail to tell him that he was no longer the boss. She picked up the telephone on his desk.

'Good morning, Felix,' she said. 'I was going to ring you in a minute.'

'It's quite all right, Maggie,' he said easily. 'I'm about to have a meeting. Before it starts, it would help if I knew whether you'd decided to accept the manager's job or not.'

'I'm sorry, Felix, but I'm going to turn it down. In fact, I've decided I'd like to do something quite different.' Hugh was staring at her, a puzzled look on his face.

'Such as?' Felix asked.

'Working with children or for a charity,' she told him.

'Good for you, Maggie. I'm sorry you're leaving us. If I hear of a job that would suit you, I'll let you know.'

'Thank you.' She put down the phone and slowly turned to Hugh. 'Before you ask, Felix offered me the job of office manager. I turned it down. I've decided that I have more important things to do with my life than work for Buzz.'

Hugh's face turned bright red and then suddenly he burst into tears. Taken aback, Maggie stammered something about wishing things had turned out better for him and left the room. Another time, she would have stayed to comfort him, but now she thought he might take it the wrong way.

Later, Hugh went out for his lunch and didn't come back. When Maggie looked in his office, she saw he'd taken the raincoat that always hung behind the door. The spare shirt that he kept in his drawer had also gone, along with the pens and books that had belonged to him. The room looked very bare.

It would appear that Hugh wasn't coming back. It seemed a sad end to the job he'd had for so many years. The way he'd behaved over the last few days wasn't a bit like the man she'd always known. Despite everything that had happened, Maggie hoped it wouldn't be long before he found another job, somewhere he would be happy.

Maggie was glad she wouldn't be working for Buzz for much longer. Felix Anderson tried to give the impression that he was really friendly. He insisted on being on first-name terms with his staff, yet the way in which he had given poor Hugh the sack was ruthless and cruel.

Carol came to say she couldn't help but overhear Maggie's conversation with Felix. 'Do you think I'd stand a chance if I applied for the manager's job?' she asked.

'There'd be nothing lost if you tried,' Maggie told her. 'Actually, Felix should have offered it to you in the first place. He only thought about me because we met in Brighton.' She remembered Hugh telling her Felix liked her. She had no idea why. 'Knowing Felix, he'll admire you for having the good sense to apply.'

Carol came back later to say she hadn't spoken to Felix. 'But his secretary told me to send an e-mail with all my details.'

'Good luck, Carol.' Maggie gave her the thumbs-up sign. 'If they ask for a reference, give them my name.'

*

That night, Maggie was in the middle of making dinner when the telephone rang. It was Tess. 'Can I come over?' she pleaded. 'I'm urgently in need of shelter.'

'Shelter?' Maggie queried.

'Shelter,' Tess confirmed. 'Susie's father has turned up. It isn't Dirk as I'd thought. This one's called Kieran, he's from Ireland, and he and Clare are having a flaming row. Olivia's crying again. Ewan's new girlfriend is here and *they're* having a row. I've forgotten what the name of my other son is.'

'Mark,' Maggie supplied. 'He's the one who's decided to hitch-hike around the world.'

'I wonder whether he has already left and that's why I can't remember him? Anyway, Mags, I need to escape from this madhouse before I go stark raving mad.'

'Come over, Tess, whenever you like. No, wait a minute. John's just rung to say he'll be home late. I'll leave his dinner in the oven and we can meet in my mother's flat. You know where it is, don't you?'

'On the waterfront not far from that big hotel? What's it called?'

'The Grand. I'll see you there in about half an hour.'

John couldn't expect her to just sit in the

house, night after night, waiting for him to come home. Maggie wrote a note and attached it to the fridge with a magnet. It said that his dinner was in the oven and he could get it out himself.

She called to Amber and together they set off for her mother's flat.

Tess arrived with an armful of bedding and two bottles of wine. She waved them in Maggie's face. 'I hope you don't mind if I spend the night here. I'll be too drunk to drive if we drink these. It'll be interesting to know if the children notice I've gone. Hello, Amber.' She patted the dog's head. 'I'd be better off with four dogs than four children.'

The women spent the evening recalling the years they'd spent together at school. They talked about the discos they'd been to and the good times they'd had, and Maggie reminded Tess about one of her boyfriends. 'He had a snake tattooed on his back. His name was Keith something.'

Tess shuddered. 'That tattoo looked horrible. What about that boyfriend of yours, Gavin Myers. He had enormous ears.'

'Gavin was born with the ears.' Maggie had quite liked Gavin. Perhaps because she was a bit drunk, she half wished that she'd married him

69

instead of John. 'Keith wasn't born with a snake tattooed on his back.'

Tess yawned. 'Don't you think you'd better be getting home, Maggie? It's nearly midnight.'

Maggie leapt to her feet. 'I didn't realise. The time's flown by. I'll leave the key with you so you can lock up whenever you leave. I'll collect it from you tomorrow on my way home from work.'

'Thanks.' Tess yawned a second time. 'John will be wondering where you are.'

'No, he won't. John will be fast asleep in bed. Come on, Amber. We're going home.'

When she let herself into the house, Maggie wondered why the lights were still on in the hall and on the stairs. She was surprised to find John in the lounge staring at the television with the sound turned down.

'I'm sorry I'm so late,' she panted. She'd rushed all the way home. 'Tess is spending the night at Mum's flat. We lost track of time. I thought you'd have gone to bed ages ago.'

John stood and faced her. She could tell by his face that something serious had happened. The hairs prickled on the back of her neck.

'I was about to go to bed when Hugh Miller arrived and said he had something important to tell me.' He paused. 'According to Hugh, you're having an affair.' He looked as if he was about to cry. 'Is it true, Margaret?'

CHAPTER 10

AMBER HAD RUSHED INTO the kitchen as soon as they'd entered the house. She came out again, sat on the floor and looked from Maggie to John, then back again. Maggie could tell she was upset about something. 'Does Amber need water in her bowl?' she asked.

'I'll check.' John disappeared into the kitchen.

Maggie wondered why her heart wasn't pounding. Why did she feel so calm? Her husband had just found out she had slept with Connor, yet it didn't seem to bother her. Today, she'd decided to give up her job and now it appeared that her marriage was about to end. Her whole world was falling apart and she didn't care.

John came back, looking at her accusingly. 'I asked if it were true, Margaret. Are you having an affair?'

'I slept with someone in Brighton,' she confessed, 'but it's all over and done with.'

'Who?' John demanded. His eyes were bright with anger. 'What's his name?'

'I'm not telling you, John. His name doesn't matter.'

For all she knew, John might turn up on Connor's doorstep and make a fuss. She was surprised that Hugh hadn't told him Connor's name.

John stuffed his hands in his pockets and began to walk up and down the room. His mouth moved, as if he was talking to himself. 'My wife has actually been to bed with another man,' he finally said aloud, as if he was trying to convince himself that it had really happened. 'I can't quite take it in, Margaret. You're the last woman I'd expect to have slept with another man.'

'I've been feeling terribly lonely, John,' she said with a sigh.

'So that's your excuse – you were lonely.' There was the touch of a sneer in his voice.

'It's not an excuse, it's the reason why it happened. I met ... the man on the Buzz weekend. He made me feel young and pretty and wanted. It's a long time since you made me feel any of those things.'

John sighed. He stopped pacing and stared at the carpet. 'I know we've grown apart,' he said.

'Why is that, do you think?' Maggie asked.

For some reason he refused to meet her eyes. 'I don't know,' he muttered. 'I need a drink. Do

73

you want one?' He went over to the sideboard and took out a half-full bottle of whisky. 'There's sherry here too.'

'No, thank you.' She'd already drunk enough that night.

'Where are the glasses?'

'In the tall cupboard in the kitchen.'

The glasses had been kept in exactly the same place ever since they'd moved into the house. Why could he not remember? He came back with the bottle in one hand and a glass in the other.

Maggie had a swift vision from the past of them being at a party somewhere. It was years and years ago, before they were married. He was much thinner then, straight-backed, curly haired, smiling. He'd gone to fetch drinks for them both. Everyone was sitting on the floor listening to the music. It was a Queen record – she'd loved Freddie Mercury even then. Maggie remembered how she had watched John step over bodies as he came towards her holding two cans of beer and her heart had swelled with love. It seemed to her that it was a miracle that, out of all the millions of people in the world, they'd found each other. He had dropped down beside her and kissed her cheek.

'I love you, Mags,' he'd murmured.

'And I love you,' she'd replied.

When had he stopped calling her Mags and begun to call her Margaret? Bit by bit he'd been distancing himself from her and now they were miles and miles apart.

She had no idea what had happened next at the party. It was just the picture of John picking his way across the room that she had treasured – that and the music. How could two people who'd loved each other so much end up as strangers?

'Would you like me to leave?' she enquired.

Some of the colour left his face. 'Do you *want* to leave?' He swallowed his drink in a single gulp.

She thought of the warmth of her mother's flat, the brilliant colours and the beautiful view. 'No,' she lied. It was bad enough that she had been unfaithful. It would be really horrible if she walked out on him as well, if he wanted her to stay.

'I thought you might want to set up home with your lover.'

'My lover!' Connor was hardly a lover. 'He's married with three children.'

John poured himself more whisky. 'Hugh said he's much younger than you.'

'He's thirty-five.' She smiled. 'He's hardly a toy boy.'

'You seem to find this very funny, Margaret,'

75

he said curtly. 'You don't seem to realise how much you've hurt me.'

'I don't find it the least bit funny, John.' She shouldn't have smiled. Having had so much wine at her mother's flat, she felt a little bit drunk. She wasn't acting normally. 'I'm sorry if I've hurt you. To tell the truth, I'm surprised you're hurt. I didn't think you would have cared that I had been unfaithful.'

'You appear to have a very low opinion of me.'

Maggie didn't know what to say. She felt hugely thirsty after drinking so much wine. She asked John whether he would like a cup of coffee or tea, but he shook his head. As she was longing for tea herself she went into the kitchen and switched on the kettle. When she came out again with her tea, there was no sign of John. She assumed that he'd gone to bed without saying goodnight.

After she'd drunk the tea, she went to bed herself. She told herself that perhaps tomorrow she'd feel bad that she'd failed John.

However, when she woke up the following morning she didn't feel the smallest bit ashamed of what she'd done.

She was getting dressed when there was a knock on the bedroom door. She shouted, 'Come in,' and John entered.

'I'm off to work now,' he said. He usually shouted to tell her that he was going from the bottom of the stairs.

'Goodbye, John.' She couldn't resist adding, 'You know, it just shows what a lousy marriage we have that we sleep in separate rooms. There's no reason for it.'

'Yes, there is,' he said coldly. 'It's because I'm a very restless sleeper. I used to keep you awake. I moved to another room for your sake.'

'I never complained,' Maggie said. 'I was quite happy with the way we were.' She'd always hated sleeping alone while knowing her husband was in the next room.

'You seem determined to put the blame for your affair on me, Margaret.' He looked hurt.

Maggie sat on the edge of the bed. She said thoughtfully, 'It *was* partly your fault, John, but it was mine too. I did nothing to stop you from shutting me out of your life. I should have put my foot down a long time ago.'

She knew that she'd been very weak. Now she had no idea how to make things better between them. It was much too late to suggest they slept together again. She couldn't very well insist that she was invited to the school pantomime or demand that she be taken to the cinema or out to dinner. Those sorts of things had to come from John himself, not her.

'We'll have a talk about it sometime,' John said. 'A long talk.'

Maggie listened to his footsteps going down the stairs and wondered whether he meant it.

CHAPTER 11

'THESE HAVE JUST COME for you, Maggie.' Carol came into the office on Thursday morning with a bunch of red roses. 'Kirsty counted them and there are twenty-four.'

'They're beautiful,' Maggie gasped. She buried her nose in the flowers – they were bound to be from Connor. 'They smell lovely.'

'There's a card with them.'

Maggie wished Carol would go away while she read the card. She couldn't think of how to explain to her who Connor was.

To her astonishment the bouquet had been sent by a most unexpected person. 'They're from Hugh!' She gasped again. Last night, Hugh had told John something that could well ruin her marriage. This morning, he was sending her flowers.

There was a message on the card. It said, 'I will never forgive myself, Hugh.' He was plainly sorry for what he'd done, though it was a bit late for that now.

'What does he have to say for himself?' Carol asked.

'I think he regrets walking out the way he

did,' Maggie said with a shrug. 'Look, would you like to put these on the counter?' She had no intention of taking them home. John would start wondering why Hugh was sending her flowers. No doubt he would suspect her of having an affair with him as well as with Connor!

'Thanks, Mags, I'll look for a vase.' A smiling Carol took the flowers away.

Five minutes later, the telephone on Maggie's desk rang. 'Are we still meeting on Sunday?' Connor asked when she picked it up.

'Y-yes,' Maggie stammered, taken by surprise.

'I can't wait,' he said excitedly, reminding her of a little boy who was looking forward to a special treat. 'See you then. Bye, Maggie.'

Maggie sat with the phone against her ear, listening to an empty humming noise. Had she done the right thing in saying yes? She wasn't sure whether she ought to see Connor on Sunday. She doubted whether she could bring herself to lie to John again.

She rested her elbows on the desk and thought hard. Her life was getting very complicated – *too* complicated. She *would* meet Connor on Sunday but it would be to tell him that they must never see each other again. It was pointless anyway. Nothing would come of it – not that she wanted it to – so she would tell him that it was time he sorted th'ngs out with Emma. There was no way that she wanted to be responsible for breaking up another woman's marriage.

On the first day at the office without Hugh, Maggie and Carol managed to run the travel agency quite smoothly between them with the help of the other girls. Hugh wasn't missed, leaving Maggie wondering what he'd done when he'd actually been there. When three o'clock came and it was time for her to leave, she asked Carol whether she'd like her to stay and help.

'No, it's all right,' she replied. 'I've got to learn to cope by myself, haven't I?'

'I suppose, though we're one member of staff short. Have you had a reply from Felix Anderson about the manager's job?'

'Not yet, Mags.' Carol grinned. 'It was only yesterday that I applied for it.'

'Was it?' So much was happening in her life that it felt as if it was weeks ago.

On the way home, Maggie called at her friend's house. She was longing to see Susie, the new baby. She also wanted to collect the keys to her mother's flat that she'd left with Tess the night before.

Olivia, Tess's youngest daughter, let her in. She was only eighteen and still at school. Her eyes were red with crying. 'Mum's in the kitchen,' she sobbed, running upstairs.

Tess was nursing a sleeping Susie while trying to use her laptop with one hand, so Maggie reached eagerly for the baby and Tess passed the child to her with a sigh of relief.

'Is Olivia still upset over losing her boyfriend?' Maggie asked.

'It would appear so,' Tess said sourly. 'She didn't go to school today and she's been playing weepy music the whole time.'

'Where's Susie's mother?'

'I'm beginning to think *I'm* Susie's mother.' Tess sounded even more sour. 'Her real mother has gone into town.'

'Surely Clare hasn't started work again already!'

'No, she's going back on Monday. Today she's gone to buy herself new clothes to fit her new slim figure.'

'Has she made arrangements to have Susie looked after while she's at work?'

'Not as far as I know,' said Tess.

Maggie could have sworn she could feel the baby's heart beating against her own. She looked down at the thick golden lashes resting on the smooth white cheek and the tiny mouth, as pink as a rose. 'She's beautiful,' she said with a throb in her voice. She would have given everything she owned in the world for a baby of her own.

Tess looked at her thoughtfully. 'I don't suppose you're looking for a job as a baby-minder?'

'Not likely.' Maggie pulled a face. 'I'd grow to love her, then one day she'd be taken away and I'd be heartbroken. I'll do some babysitting now and again, but that's all.'

Tess's glum face brightened. 'I'll tell you what you could do, Mags. You could let Clare have your mother's flat. I told her all about it when I got home this morning. I think she and Kieran might get together if they had a place of their own.'

'Who's Kieran?'

Tess rolled her eyes impatiently. 'I told you on the phone last night, he's Susie's father and he comes from Dublin. He was really cross that Clare hadn't told him she was expecting a baby. It seems he quite likes the idea of being a dad.'

Maggie shook her head. 'I'm sorry, Tess, but I want to keep Mum's flat.'

'What for?' Tess demanded. 'It's of no use to you. If Clare and Kieran were living together then she might stay home and look after Susie and I'd be off the hook.'

'I can't let the flat because I might need it for myself one day.'

Tess looked at her, astounded. 'What do you mean by that?'

'Exactly what I said.' Maggie explained what had happened the night before. 'When I got home, John was still up. Hugh Miller had been to the house and told him about Connor.'

'Hugh Miller is an idiot,' Tess said scornfully. 'I've never liked him.'

'Anyway,' Maggie continued, 'John asked whether I was going to leave, but I told him that I wasn't.' She stroked Susie's face with her finger. 'I'm not really sure whether I meant it, but I realised for the first time that I wasn't in love with John any more. I'll wait and see what happens. One of these days I could well move into Mum's flat myself. I'll tell you what,' she said, 'if I'm not living there by Christmas, then Clare and Kieran can have it.' She smiled down at the baby in her arms. 'And Susie.'

She visited the flat on her way home. It felt warm, despite the fact that the heating wasn't on. By now it was dark and she sat in the window, watching the traffic go by. She could hear music, something classical, coming from the flat on the top floor.

All of a sudden, without warning, Maggie began to cry. She cried and cried until her chest and stomach hurt. She hadn't wanted to fall out of love with John. When they married, she'd imagined them staying together always. 'Till death do us part,' the vicar had said.

She thought of the cold, dull house in Crosby where she'd spent twelve cold, dull years. How different it would be if the house were full of children – their noise, their toys and possessions, their friends.

But it was not to be. She couldn't imagine her and John making love again – anyway, she was probably much too old now to have a baby. At that thought, Maggie began to cry even more.

CHAPTER 12

NEXT DAY, MAGGIE HAD a visitor. She'd hardly been in the office more than ten minutes when Carol announced there was a Mrs Bailey to see her.

'Is it about a holiday?' Maggie asked.

Carol shrugged. 'I've no idea. She just asked for you. I didn't like to ask what it was about.'

Mrs Bailey was tall and stout. Her hair was iron-grey with white streaks and it stuck out like a halo around her rosy face. She wore a red suit, which clashed horribly with her pink blouse. Maggie liked her twinkling eyes and broad smile. They shook hands and Maggie asked her to sit down.

'You're probably wondering why I'm here,' Mrs Bailey began. 'Oh, before we go any further, my name is Olive. Is it all right if I call you Maggie?'

'Of course – Olive.'

'I'm here because Felix Anderson told me you're looking for a job. A part-time job with a charity and working with children. He appears to think very highly of you.'

'I am looking for a job, yes.' She had no idea

what she'd done to make Felix Anderson think so highly of her.

'Well, I have a job that would suit you right down to the ground,' Mrs Bailey – Olive – said with her lovely smile. 'First of all, I must explain that I can't offer it to you here and now. The decision has to go before a committee and we have a couple of other applicants to see. It's just that I happened to be in Liverpool and thought I'd pop in. I'm actually based in Manchester, you see.'

'What sort of job is it?' Maggie asked.

'Well, dear, I'm the North-West area organiser of NOMA. That stands for No More Aids. Our job is to raise funds for research into a cure for Aids. NOMA was founded by Felix Anderson – did you know he had a young brother who died from Aids?'

'No, I didn't,' Maggie murmured.

'He's such a dear man, Felix,' Olive gushed. 'His generosity knows no bounds.'

Olive had only seen the good side of Felix Anderson, Maggie thought – and he did have a good side, that was gradually becoming clear.

'The job requires someone who is able to work from home. Would that suit you, Maggie?'

'Yes,' Maggie said, though she wasn't really sure whether she wanted to work at home.

'And do you have a computer?'

'Yes,' she said again. It was in the spare bedroom. John used it sometimes, but Maggie hardly ever touched it. She had enough of computers at work. 'And what exactly would I do?' she enquired. 'If I got the job, that is,' she added hastily.

'Oh, I haven't told you, have I? We need a fund-raiser,' Olive announced. 'To start with, he or she will write to every single person and company in this area who might be willing to make a donation to NOMA. There are loads and loads of other ways of raising money. I'm sure you'll think of some yourself.'

'Do you have a Christmas gift catalogue?' Maggie asked.

'No, but that's a very good idea,' Olive said thoughtfully. 'It's too late for this year, but perhaps we could start putting one together for next year. However, we have just started a Christmas raffle and you would be expected to find the prizes for next year's. We've already got this year's.'

'How would I do that – find the prizes?'

'Easily, dear,' Olive assured her. 'Some garages will be happy to donate a car as long as the people who buy tickets know where it came from. There are times when it's more helpful to use the direct approach. In other words, call personally rather than telephone or e-mail. You can always claim expenses.'

Maggie gulped at the idea of calling in at a garage out of the blue and asking for a car for nothing. She watched as Olive rooted through her handbag and produced a thick wad of raffle tickets.

'I've brought a dozen books of this year's tickets with me,' she explained. 'I expect you could sell them to the other staff.'

'I'll do my best,' Maggie promised. She'd never liked asking people to buy tickets.

This must have been obvious in her voice. Olive put a finger to her plump chin and regarded her thoughtfully. 'I wonder whether you've got the right attitude for this job, Maggie? You need to be as hard as nails and have a skin like an elephant. Aids is a touchy subject for some people. I've had quite a few folk tell me that anyone with Aids has only got what they deserved. Of course, Princess Diana helped make it more acceptable, but sadly she's no longer with us.'

'I'm sure I could cope.' Until then, Maggie hadn't been sure whether she wanted the job. Now that Olive had suggested that she had the wrong attitude, she wanted it badly. It sounded challenging and she just knew she would enjoy it. 'I can grow a skin like an elephant very quickly,' she said.

Olive beamed as she got to her feet. 'Good girl! I'll let you know as soon as a decision is made. Out of interest, when could you start?'

'If it was up to me, I'd start tomorrow. As it is, I feel I should wait until they get someone to take over my job here.'

'If that's the case, I can speak to Felix. He'll sort it out.' She spoke as if there was nothing on earth that Felix Anderson couldn't do.

That afternoon, rather than go home after work, Maggie walked down to the Pier Head. Although there was a chill in the air, the sun blazed down from a clear blue sky and the waters of the River Mersey shone like silver.

A ferry was just leaving on its way to New Brighton. When she was a small child, her mum and dad had taken her to the fairground there on Sundays when Dad was home from sea. He'd taken her on the merry-go-round with him. He'd sat on the back of the horse while she sat on the front, and she'd felt safe and secure in his strong arms.

After the fairground, they'd go to a café and have fish and chips. Since then, Maggie hadn't eaten many meals that tasted as good as those fish and chips.

A voice said, 'Hello there, Maggie.' She turned to find Hugh Miller standing beside her. He looked wretched.

'Have you been following me?' she asked angrily.

'No, I was watching the ferries. My parents used to bring my brother and me here on Sundays after church.' He smiled sadly. 'That was more years ago than I care to remember.'

'I'm amazed you've got the nerve to talk to me. That was a really horrible thing you did on Wednesday night.'

'I know and I'm sorry. I wished I hadn't done it as soon as I came out of your house. I hardly slept all night because I felt so ashamed.' He looked so unhappy that Maggie actually felt pity for him, despite the awful thing he'd done. 'How are things between you and John?' he asked.

'Not good,' she said, shrugging. 'But then they haven't been good for a long time.'

'I suppose I've made them worse,' he said glumly.

'Possibly.' She wasn't all that sure how John really felt about her sleeping with another man.

'Did you get the flowers?'

'Yes, thank you. They were very nice. You know, Hugh,' she said, looking at him irritably, 'I thought you and I were friends.'

'So did I, Mags. I'm sorry I let you down. I only did it because I was jealous.' He looked at her sorrowfully. 'Can we be friends again?'

How could she refuse a request like that? 'Oh, all right,' she said.

'Perhaps we could see each other now and then, go to dinner, maybe. There'd be nothing romantic about it,' he assured her. 'We'd be friends, that's all. I'm badly in need of a friend at the moment.' He smiled dryly. 'In fact, you're the only one I've got.'

'All right,' she said again.

As if to prove she had the right attitude for the fund-raising job with NOMA, Maggie sold him two books of raffle tickets.

John arrived home late as usual. He seemed a bit distant, but that was all, and Maggie assumed that their rather empty marriage would survive her short but sweet affair with Connor.

She told John over dinner about the job interview she'd had that day. She hadn't realised until then that he didn't know Felix Anderson had offered her the position of office manager in place of Hugh.

'You forgot to tell me.' He actually had the nerve to look annoyed. 'Why didn't you tell me about it before you turned it down?'

'Why? Would you have talked me into taking it?'

'Of course not. It's just that it's something I would have expected you to discuss with me.'

'Huh!' She was so cross that she sprinkled too much pepper on her dinner. 'I can't recall you discussing with me the conference that you went to in Blackpool. Or the one in Leeds. You just told me you were going, that's all. You never discuss with me anything that goes on in school.'

'You're right, I'm sorry,' he said humbly. 'Things are going to be different from now on.'

Before Maggie went to bed, she looked in the spare bedroom where the computer was kept along with a few boxes of ornaments and old books that should have been put in the loft. The only furniture was the desk, where the computer stood, and a chair. The walls were painted cream and the window overlooked the side of the house next door, facing a similar window with a green blind, which was pulled down. The view was as miserable as sin. It wasn't exactly a pleasant room to work in.

Amber had come with her, but she sniffed, turned and walked out again. It seemed she didn't like the room either.

Maggie imagined being in a different room

altogether. In that room, the window had a fantastic view of the River Mersey. It was made cheerful by old comfortable furniture and bright colours. If she got the job with NOMA, that was where she wanted to work, not here.

CHAPTER 13

On Sunday, Maggie found Connor sitting at the same table in the Life Café as when she had met him a week earlier. They were the only people in the upstairs area. When he saw her, he jumped to his feet and kissed her.

When they sat down facing each other, she said quickly, 'I can't do this any more, Connor. I hate telling lies to my husband. He thinks I've gone shopping.'

Connor took both her hands in his. 'I feel just as bad,' he said. 'I told Emma I was seeing some people I'd met on the Buzz weekend to discuss skiing holidays. I guess we're not cut out for affairs, Maggie.'

Maggie agreed. 'I don't think we are.'

'Does that mean this is the last time we'll see each other?'

'I think that would be best, don't you?'

His handsome face fell. 'You're right, it would.' He squeezed her hands tightly. 'I won't ever forget you, Maggie.'

'And I won't forget you.' She knew he would always have a place in her heart.

A waitress came and took their order for

coffee. They held hands while they waited for it to come. Now that they realised they would never meet again, every remaining moment felt precious. Maggie studied Connor's face, every little detail of it. She was storing it in her head so that she would never forget what he looked like, and Connor was looking at her in the same way.

Neither knew much about the other. Maggie told him about her mum, and about her dad who had died when she was five. 'He was a merchant seaman.' She described her mother's flat. 'One of these days I might go and live there.'

Connor's own father had died before he was born and his mother had handed over his care to his grandfather. 'He was a bad-tempered old thing, but I really loved him.' Connor had met his wife, Emma, at school. 'I was sixteen and she was fourteen. It's funny, but we didn't like each other much at first.'

'John and I fell in love straightaway. He was still at university and I was working as a typist in a bank.' She would never understand how much their feelings for each other had changed in the years between.

Connor's mobile phone rang. He frowned and took it out of the pocket of his leather jacket. 'Excuse me, Maggie. Hello,' he said into the phone.

She sat quietly, watching him.

'*What!*' he shouted a few seconds later. He listened intently, then snapped, 'I'll be there in an hour's time.' He turned back to Maggie. 'That was the hospital,' he said abruptly. 'Emma's had an accident in the car. She had one of the children with her – it can only be Harry. I know that my mother-in-law took Kate and Charlie to the cinema today.'

'Oh, Connor, I'm so sorry,' Maggie cried. 'Are they badly hurt?'

'Emma was knocked unconscious, that's all the doctor would say.' He got to his feet. 'I've got to go, Maggie.'

'Of course you have.' Maggie stood too. 'Shall I come with you to the car?'

'No, thank you, it'll be quicker if I go alone.'

They embraced for the very last time and, before Maggie knew it, Connor had gone out of her life for ever.

She had no idea how long she sat alone at the table. When the waitress came to collect the cups, she ordered more coffee. She felt as lonely now as she had on the first night in Brighton when she'd met Connor. A light had gone out of her life that would never be lit again.

97

When she looked at her watch, an entire hour had passed. Connor should be in Manchester by now.

Laughter came from downstairs in the café. She was seated on the balcony overlooking the ground floor and the laughter came from a table below where a couple sat with three children. Why hadn't *she* had children? Every woman deserved to have children. Tears trickled down her cheeks. It wasn't fair.

A telephone rang, making her jump. It was Connor's mobile. He'd gone in such a hurry that he'd left it behind. Perhaps he'd just discovered it was missing and was calling from another phone. She picked it up and said, 'Hello.'

'Oh!' said a young woman's voice. 'I was expecting Connor to answer.'

'He's gone, I'm afraid,' Maggie explained. 'He had to rush back because his wife had had an accident and he forgot to take his mobile with him.'

'I'm his wife. I'm Emma. I just wanted to let him know I'm all right now.'

'I'm so pleased,' Maggie said warmly, 'he was terribly worried about you. He should be there any minute now. The hospital said that one of the children was with you in the car.'

'It's Harry. He's fine. Oh, I must tell you,'

Emma said in a rush. 'I'm so proud. I skidded off the road into a ditch and knocked myself out. Harry was in the car seat at the back. He not only managed to undo himself, but he also climbed on to the front seat and dialled 999 on my mobile. He's only three. Everyone in the hospital thinks he's a hero. One of the nurses has contacted the local paper and someone's coming to take his photograph.'

'He sounds a very clever little boy,' Maggie said.

'Doesn't he!' Emma sounded pleased. 'I didn't realise until today. He so often gets on my nerves, asking questions all the time, but he's a good boy really. From now on, I shall be more patient with him.'

'I'm glad everything's turned out well for you.' Maybe now Emma would realise what a lucky woman she was.

'Oh, here's Connor! I can see him through the window. His car has just driven into the car park. Thank you for talking to me – what's your name?'

'Margaret Holt.'

'Are you one of the people who Connor met on that weekend in Brighton?'

'Yes, I work for a travel agent in Liverpool. A group of us decided to meet now and then to discuss business.'

'And here's me holding up your meeting while I chatter on. I'm so sorry, Margaret.'

'It's all right,' Maggie said in a sad voice. 'I was about to leave. The meeting's over.'

CHAPTER 14

MAGGIE WAS ON HER way home when Connor's mobile rang again. She stopped the car and picked it up. This time it really was him.

'I'm calling from the hospital,' he said. 'Emma said she'd spoken to you.'

'Yes. She sounds very nice, Connor.'

'She is. I don't quite know what went wrong between us.' He sighed.

'Whatever it is, you must both do your best to put it right,' Maggie advised. If only she and John had tried to sort out their problems a long time ago, they might not have reached the stage they were at now.

'I'm just on my way to collect Harry,' Connor said. 'He's in the children's ward having his photo taken – it seems he's quite a celebrity – then we're going home.'

'What shall I do with your mobile?' she enquired.

'Send it to the agency. I'll e-mail you the address.'

'I'll post it tomorrow,' she promised. 'I hope everything goes well for you and Emma, Connor. Have a lovely life,' she said softly.

'You too, my dear, dear Maggie.'

They rang off and Maggie sat for a minute with her forehead resting on the steering wheel. Then she straightened up, pulled back her shoulders and started the engine. She couldn't face going home to her miserable house, so she would go to her mother's welcoming flat instead.

The clocks had gone back the week before so it was dark by the time she arrived. She let herself into the house and climbed the stairs to the flat.

She unlocked the flat door and went inside, but froze when she saw a strip of light shining from underneath the bedroom door. Someone was in there!

Had Tess returned in search of more peace? But she'd collected the keys from Tess the night before, so she wouldn't have been able to get in. The only other set of keys for the flat were at home in one of the drawers in the kitchen.

Had John come there for some reason? Well, the only way of finding out was to open the bedroom door and see.

She grasped the handle, pushed the door open and nearly died of surprise when she came face to face with a completed naked John. His face went as white as a sheet when he saw her. 'I thought I heard a noise,' he said in a cracked voice. 'What on earth are you doing here, Margaret?'

'There's no need to ask *you* that question, John. It's obvious what you're doing.' Maggie turned towards the woman sitting up in her mother's bed. 'Mrs Granger, isn't it? I think you teach history – or do you give sex lessons?' Mrs Granger was a very glamorous forty-year-old. Maggie couldn't remember her first name, but she was already teaching at the school when John became headmaster. 'How long has this been going on?' she demanded.

Neither answered. Mrs Granger held the duvet in front of her, but it was obvious she was naked too. Maggie was horrified when she was overcome with an urge to laugh.

'I'll see you at home, Margaret,' John said, pulling on his trousers. Mrs Granger, who hadn't moved from the bed, looked as if she was glued to it. 'I'd expected you to go straight there from your shopping trip.'

Maggie remembered she'd told him she was going to town again to look for a winter coat. 'I felt like coming here instead,' she said.

Without another word, she turned on her heel and left the flat. Once again, she didn't go home, but drove to Tess's house. Today had been one of the strangest days of her life. She'd met Connor for the last time. Emma had had an accident. Now she'd found John in bed with one of the teachers from his school. They would surely be dismissed if they were found out.

'Well, who would have believed it!' Tess remarked when Maggie told her about John and Mrs Granger. Tess was in the kitchen, puffing away on a cigarette.

'Don't tell anyone, will you?' Maggie pleaded. 'I don't want to get them into trouble.'

'You're too nice for your own good, Maggie,' Tess said with a sniff. 'Too nice for John, at any rate.'

'I slept with Connor, didn't I?' Maggie pointed out. 'I'm just as bad in my own way.'

'You wouldn't have done it if you'd been happy with John, would you?'

'Well, no,' Maggie admitted.

'He and this Mrs Granger bitch might have been having an affair for ages.'

'I suppose,' Maggie sighed. 'Why is every-where so quiet?' There was a surprising lack of noise in the house.

'They're all out. Clare and Kieran have taken Susie to Dublin to meet his parents. I've got a feeling they might stay there. Kieran's folks are really well off.'

'Won't you mind?' Maggie asked.

'I'll miss Susie, naturally, but I expect I'll have plenty more grandchildren. Olivia's out with a new boyfriend, Ewan's out with his latest fiancée, and Mark really *has* decided to hitch-hike around the world. Mind you, I'm expecting him back any minute – if Mark doesn't have a shower and clean underpants every day, he'll die.'

'Does that mean you've got a bed to spare?'

'Yes.' Tess grinned. 'Do you want it?'

'Please. I'm not in the mood to listen to John tonight, explaining what he was doing in bed with Mrs Granger.' She wasn't sure whether she'd be upset or laugh!

Just after eight, the telephone rang. 'If it's John, tell him I'm having a shower and I'll see him tomorrow after school,' she said to Tess.

It was indeed John, who sounded very unhappy, Tess reported, after she'd given him Maggie's message.

'He deserves to be unhappy,' Maggie said. At the same time, she couldn't help but feel sorry for him.

Next morning, she stayed at Tess's house until she was confident that John would have left for work. There would just be time for her to wash and change into fresh clothes before she went

MAUREEN LEE

to Astral. Today would be the start of her last week with the agency. Felix Anderson had arranged for a woman from Head Office to take charge for a few weeks, and to decide whether Carol was capable of taking over the manager's job.

She felt cross when she arrived at the house and saw John's car still in the drive. He must be going into school late just so that he could talk to her first. She'd never known him be late before.

'I was beginning to get worried when you didn't come home last night,' he said when she walked into the house. 'That's why I called Tess.' To her great surprise, he took her in his arms. 'Darling! I'm so terribly sorry. Are you very upset by what happened?'

Maggie was even more surprised by her lack of feeling. 'No, not really.'

It was John's turn to look surprised. 'I took it for granted that I'd hurt you badly.'

'You hurt me badly a long time ago, John.' She twisted out of his arms. 'I've sort of got used to it. I don't think you can hurt me ever again.' All those years of sleeping apart, of him ignoring her, of seeing him for only an hour or so every day. It all fitted together with a terrible clarity. 'Is Mrs Granger the reason why you stopped inviting me to the pantomime and

106

other events at the school? Is she the real reason we've been sleeping in separate beds for years now?'

He hung his head. There was a long silence. 'Not really,' he said at last. 'I just got so involved with the school that I had no time for anything else, not even you, Maggie. Jennifer Granger was there. She understood. Before I knew it, we were sleeping together.'

What made him think that *she* wouldn't have understood if he'd explained the pressure he was under? 'Do you want to marry her?' Maggie asked bluntly.

'No, Margaret.' There was a look of panic in his eyes. 'I want to stay married to you.'

'Why?'

'Because I love you.'

'You've got a funny way of showing it, John. How long have you and Mrs Granger been having an affair?'

There was a scratching at the back door so Maggie went to let Amber in.

'Five years,' John said when she came back. His face went red with shame.

'*Five years!* – and you don't want to marry her?'

'I don't want to lose you, Margaret.'

'I'm sorry, John, but you've already lost me. I think you lost me a long, long time ago.'

Maggie turned and went upstairs. It was over, *really* over. She should have left him years before. Connor had made her realise that she was still an attractive woman. He had also shown her that it was possible to be happy again. She recalled that John had been annoyed when he'd heard she'd slept with another man, yet he'd been having an affair with Jennifer Granger for five years. No wonder he always looked so tired. What a hypocrite he was!

She was working away in her office when Olive Bailey telephoned to say she'd got the job with NOMA. 'You were by far the best candidate,' she said. 'Do you know yet when you can start?'

'Will next Monday do?'

'Next Monday would be marvellous. I'll come and see you at your home if that's all right.'

'That's fine. I look forward to seeing you.'

Maggie's life was so confused just then that she wasn't sure how she felt about the job with NOMA. It wasn't until she put down the phone that she realised she was thrilled to bits.

CHAPTER 15

IT WAS CHRISTMAS MORNING. The first thing that Maggie did when she got up was to switch on the tree lights. The little coloured bulbs shone between the strips of tinsel and the silver branches, making everything glitter and gleam. Maggie could remember some of the decorations from her childhood and they brought back lovely memories of times gone by. The tree was in the same corner of the flat where her mother always used to put it.

Through the window she could see that snow was falling, but the central heating had been on all night and the flat was lovely and warm. Amber raised her head from her basket by the tree and gave Maggie a soft little bark.

'And a Merry Christmas to you too,' Maggie said.

She returned to the bedroom to put on jeans and a lime-green sweatshirt, then went to the kitchen where she made a pot of tea. She sat in front of the window to drink the first cup. A little boy rode past on what was obviously a new bike that Father Christmas must have brought for him. The tyres made black lines in the snow. A girl a bit younger followed pushing a smart pram, looking very important, and their mother and father walked behind, their arms linked.

A few months ago, the sight would have made Maggie feel envious, but not now.

She was expecting a baby. It was due to arrive the following year in the middle of July and she didn't care whether it was a boy or a girl.

No one knew except the doctor, Olive Bailey and Tess. Maggie put her cup on the floor and placed her hands flat on her tummy. It was much too soon, but she kept praying that the baby would start to kick. It would make him or her seem more real.

Her baby! If it were a boy, she would call him Connor after his father, though Connor would never know he had another child. She would call a girl Marianne after her mother.

The telephone rang. It was John, wishing her a Merry Christmas and asking whether he could come in a minute to take Amber for a walk.

'That would be nice. Thank you, John.'

They shared the dog between them. Some days Amber spent with Maggie and others with John, who so far was being very nice. Maggie had no idea whether he was still seeing Jennifer Granger – apart from at school, that is. She had a feeling that he wanted her to come back home, but knew she never would. She was happy being on her own in the place where her mum had lived, and she would be even happier when her baby came. Olive Bailey had assured her she wouldn't have to give up her job with NOMA because she was a mother. The desk with the computer was right in front of the window and she could watch the river while she worked.

The telephone rang again. This time it was Tess wishing her a Happy Christmas.

'And the same to you too,' Maggie replied.

'Don't forget, I'm expecting you for Christmas lunch at three o'clock,' Tess reminded her. 'All the kids will be here with their boyfriends and girlfriends.'

'As if I'd forget something like that!' It was going to be a lovely day. She was really looking forward to it.

She was on her way to get more tea when there was a knock on the door. It was Ben Taylor, the man from the top-floor flat who was an expert in computers. He wished her a Merry Christmas and held up a gaily wrapped parcel.

'It's a present for looking after Socks,' he said.

'I didn't expect anything,' Maggie cried. Socks was his cat, black with four white paws, and Maggie had fed her while Ben had gone away on a course. 'Would you like a cup of tea?'

'I wouldn't say no.'

He came into the room and watched while she opened the parcel – a bottle of Paris, her favourite perfume. 'Thank you very much.' She sprayed some behind her ears and sniffed. 'It's lovely.'

'Are you going downstairs for a drink at midday?' he asked.

'Of course.'

Sofia, the girl on the ground floor who liked Freddie Mercury, was having a drinks party, although now that she was pregnant, Maggie intended drinking only orange juice.

Everyone in the house was very friendly – it was like being part of a big family. The couple on the floor above had gone away, but would be home again to host a party on New Year's Eve.

Ben left and a few minutes later John arrived to take Amber for a walk. 'Shall I keep her for the rest of the day?' he asked.

'I think she'd like that,' Maggie said. 'She misses you when she's here.'

John smiled. 'She misses you when she's with me. I think she would like us both to be together again.'

Maggie didn't say that there was no chance

of that. She no longer loved John, but she liked him and didn't want to hurt him.

She watched through the window as Amber dragged John along the road, keen to get back to her old home. Perhaps she expected Maggie to be there when she arrived.

It turned out to be a magical day. The party downstairs was good fun and when Ben asked whether he could take her to dinner on Boxing Day, she agreed. She hoped he didn't have any romantic notions. Right now, Connor was the only man she had room for in her heart and she couldn't imagine ever becoming involved with someone else.

Tess's house was full of laughter. Clare and Kieran were living in Dublin now, but had brought Susie home to stay with her grand-mother at Christmas. The young couple were getting married in the new year. Susie was nearly three months old and never stopped smiling.

After lunch, they all played 'Charades' and 'Who Wants to be a Millionaire?' until tea-time when the young people went on to a party. Susie was put to bed, and Maggie and Tess watched *Gone With the Wind* on television. It was nearly four hours long and by the time it ended they were both in tears.

113

When she got back to the flat, Maggie switched on just the tree lights so that the room was lit only by little red, yellow, blue and green twinkling stars. It looked a bit ghostly. She tiptoed across the room to the oval mirror where her mum had always claimed she could see Maggie's father.

For the first time, Maggie could have sworn she could see him now. His eyes were grey like hers and he had a little beard. Then her father faded and she could see her mother instead.

'Hello, Mum,' she whispered.

Mum smiled and, as she went away, another man appeared. It was Connor, the father of her child.

Tears came to Maggie's eyes and she touched the mirror with her finger. Suddenly, all she could see was herself and a glow spread through her, moving from the top of her head right down to the tips of her toes. She smiled and felt as if she was about to burst with happiness, though she knew that not every day would be as wonderful as this one. She had to be prepared for the bad times as well as the good.

But right now, all she could think of was that by the time next Christmas came, she would be a mother.

It really was like a dream come true.

READ ON THE BEACH!
Win a holiday to Barbados

Fly to the beautiful four-star **Amaryllis Beach Resort** set on a white, sandy beach on the south coast of Barbados.

For more information about the resort please visit www.amaryllisbeachresort.com. letsgo2.com

Other prizes to be won

- **£100-worth of books for all the family**
  (we have five sets to give away)

- **A limousine for an evening in London**

- **£100-worth of M&S vouchers**
  (we have two sets to give away)

HOW TO ENTER

Fill in the form below.

Name two authors who have written Quick Reads books:

1. _____

2. _____

Your name: _____

Address: _____

_____

Telephone number: _____

Tell us where you heard about Quick Reads: _____

_____

☐ **I have read and agree to the terms and conditions on the back of this page**

Send this form to: Quick Reads Competition, Colman Getty, 28 Windmill Street, London, W1T 2JJ or enter the competition on our website www.quickreads.org.uk.
Closing date: 1 September 2007

QUICK READS COMPETITION

TERMS AND CONDITIONS

1. You must be aged 18 years or older and resident in the UK to enter this competition. If you or an immediate family member works or is otherwise involved in the Quick Reads initiative or in this promotion, you may not enter.

2. To enter, fill in the entry form in the back of a Quick Reads book, in ink or ballpoint pen, tear it out and send it to: Quick Reads Competition, Colman Getty, 28 Windmill Street, London W1T 2JJ before the closing date of 1 September 2007. Or enter on our website at www.quickreads.org.uk before 1 September 2007.

3. You may enter as many times as you wish. Each entry must be on a separate form found in the back of a Quick Reads book or a separate entry on the www.quickreads.org.uk website. No entries will be returned.

4. By entering this competition you agree to the terms and conditions.

5. We cannot be responsible for entry forms lost, delayed or damaged in the post. Proof of posting is not accepted as proof of delivery.

6. The prizes will be awarded to the people who have answered the competition questions correctly and whose entry forms are drawn out first, randomly, by an independent judge after the closing date. We will contact the winners by telephone by 1 November 2007.

7. There are several prizes:
   First Prize (there will be one first prize-winner) – Seven nights' stay at a four-star resort in Barbados. The holiday is based on two people sharing a self-catering studio room with double or twin beds and includes: return flights from a London airport, seven nights' accommodation (excludes meals), use of the resort gym and non-motorised water sports. Travel to and from the London airport is not included. You will be responsible for airport transfers, visa, passport and insurance requirements, vaccinations (if applicable), passenger taxes, charges, fees and surcharges (the amount of which is subject to change). You must travel before 1 May 2008. You must book at least four weeks before departure and bookings will be strictly subject to availability. The prize-winner will be bound by the conditions of booking issued by the operator.
   Second Prize (there will be five second prize-winners) – A set of books selected by the competition Promoter including books suitable for men, women and children – to be provided by Quick Reads up to the retail value of £100.
   Third Prize (there will be one third prize-winner) – An evening in a limousine travelling around London between the hours of 6 p.m. and midnight in a limousine provided by us. You and up to five other people will be collected from any one central London point and can travel anywhere within inner London. Champagne is included. Travel to and from London is not included.
   Fourth Prize (there will be two fourth prize-winners) – £100-worth of Marks & Spencer vouchers to be spent in any branch of M&S.

8. There is no cash alternative for any of these prizes and unless agreed otherwise in writing the prizes are non-refundable and non-transferable.

9. The Promoter reserves the right to vary, amend, suspend or withdraw any or all of the prizes if this becomes necessary for reasons beyond its control.

10. The names and photographs of prize-winners may be used for publicity by the Promoter, provided they agree at the time.

11. Details of prize-winners' names and counties will be available for one month after the close of the promotion by writing to the Promoter at the address set out below.

12. The Promoter, its associated companies and agents, exclude responsibility for any act or failure by any third-party supplier, including airlines, hotels or travel companies, as long as this is within the law. Therefore this does not apply to personal injury or negligence.

13. The Promoter is Quick Reads/World Book Day Limited, 272 Vauxhall Bridge Road, London SW1V 1BA.

Quick Reads
Pick up a book today

Quick Reads are published alongside and in partnership with BBC RaW.

We would like to thank all our partners in the Quick Reads project for their help and support:

NIACE
unionlearn
National Book Tokens
The Vital Link
The Reading Agency
National Literacy Trust
Booktrust
Welsh Books Council
The Basic Skills Agency, Wales
Accent Press
Communities Scotland

Quick Reads would also like to thank the Department for Education and Skills, Arts Council England and World Book Day for their sponsorship, and NIACE (the National Institute for Adult Continuing Education) for their outreach work.

Quick Reads is a World Book Day initiative.

Quick Reads

Books in the Quick Reads series

New titles

A Dream Come True	Maureen Lee
Burning Ambition	Allen Carr
Lily	Adèle Geras
Made of Steel	Terrance Dicks
Reading My Arse	Ricky Tomlinson
The Sun Book of Short Stories	
Survive the Worst and Aim for the Best	Kerry Katona
Twenty Tales from the War Zone	John Simpson

Backlist

Blackwater	Conn Iggulden
Book Boy	Joanna Trollope
Chickenfeed	Minette Walters
Cleanskin	Val McDermid
Danny Wallace and the Centre of the Universe	Danny Wallace
Don't Make Me Laugh	Patrick Augustus
The Grey Man	Andy McNab
Hell Island	Matthew Reilly
How to Change Your Life in Seven Steps	John Bird
I Am a Dalek	Gareth Roberts
The Name You Once Gave Me	Mike Phillips
Star Sullivan	Maeve Binchy

Don't get by get on 0800 100 900

We provide courses for anyone who wants to develop their skills. All courses are free and are available in your local area. If you'd like to find out more, phone 0800 100 900.

First Choice Books

If you enjoyed this Quick Reads book, you'll find more great reads on www.firstchoicebooks.org.uk or at your local library.

First Choice is part of The Vital Link, promoting reading for pleasure. To find out more about The Vital Link visit www.vitallink.org.uk.

Find out what the BBC's RaW (Reading and Writing Campaign) has to offer at www.bbc.co.uk/raw.

Quick Reads

Lily: A Ghost Story
by Adèle Geras

Orion

'My name is Marie Cotter and I want you to believe me. Every word of this story is true . . .'

Seventeen-year-old Marie has had a lot to cope with in her young life. But things are getting better, especially when she gets a job working for the widower, Dr Slade, looking after his four-year-old daughter, Amy.

At first, her new job seems perfect. Marie loves Amy, and Amy seems to like Marie too. Then things start to change. It seems that not everyone is happy with the new arrangement. There appears to be someone else in the house – someone who is determined to come between Amy and Marie . . .